PERSIAN PENALTY

PET WHISPERER P.I.
BOOK 14

MOLLY FITZ

ABOUT THIS BOOK

We've finally found my long-lost grandmother, and I refuse to wait another day to meet her in person. Unfortunately, she's proving rather difficult to pin down.

So Charles and I decide to finish our search on the ground and book a quirky lakeside B&B to serve as our HQ while we're in the area.

But because nothing is ever easy, we stumble across mystery after mystery while simply trying to get a good night's sleep. Precious items from our luggage keep going missing, the door to our room won't close properly, and bad reviews online hint at even worse things to come. Of course, the ill-tempered proprietress and her even crazier Persian cat refuse to help—or even to apologize.

All of which makes me wonder, will I finally get to meet my missing grandma face-to-face, or could the trouble at the inn have us packing our bags long before then?

1

'm Angie Russo, and my life has never been normal. My family is full of superstars, most notably my nan, who once stole the stage on Broadway and is to this day the most memorable character you'll ever meet. For the longest time, I searched for what would make me special, too. I guess that's why I racked up seven associate degrees before finally settling into a career.

My calling was actually a cat call—no, not the sleazy, random-guy-on-the-street kind. An actual *meow*. A meow that I heard loud and clear, and in English of all things.

Yes, I can talk to animals. Just call me Miss Dolittle.

I was working as a paralegal when a will meeting went awry. One thing led to another, and I got zapped by a faulty coffee maker, lost consciousness, and then eventually woke up with a talking cat on my chest.

And, boy, did he have a lot of demands!

Fast-forward a couple years, and now he's my partner in the P.I. business. Thanks in large part to his former owner, his name is Octavius Maxwell Ricardo Edmund Frederick Fulton Russo, Esq, P.I. Since that's way longer than any honest name should be, I've taken to calling him Octo-Cat.

Together, we live in a beautiful manor home not too far from Blueberry Bay in Maine. Nan lives with us, too, as does her syrupy sweet rescue Chihuahua, Paisley. Our backyard neighbor is a sticky-fingered raccoon named Pringle; he helps us occasionally and bribes us regularly.

Never a dull moment with this colorful cast of sidekicks.

Of course, I'd be remiss if I failed to mention Charles Longfellow, III. He's the senior partner at a local law firm, the same one I used to work at back in the day. He's my boyfri—I mean, *fiancé!*

He's my fiancé!

Wow, I still haven't gotten used to saying that.

He proposed to me on a surprise weekend getaway that came with a rented RV and a crazy murder mystery. It was supposed to help me relax, but I'm honestly more wound up than ever.

Not just because of the proposal, but also because of what happened after we returned home.

A few months ago I made a deal to help some seagulls with an inter-flock dispute. In exchange, they promised to find my long-lost grandmother, whom I only knew about thanks to a hidden letter Pringle filched from the attic.

Nan—my best friend and the woman who raised me while my parents were busy focusing on their careers and each other—well, it turns out she's not actually blood related.

I'm still getting over the shock from that particular revelation!

Needless to say, Nan has had a rough time accepting that I want to connect to the grandmother I never knew. I've taken every opportunity I can to reassure her, but it's still hard. She didn't choose for her best friend—my blood grandfather—to hand her his baby and ask her to run. Nan never asked why, and he died before I could suss out any answers. That leaves my long-lost grandmother as the only one who can explain why things happened the way they did.

I've got to find her and learn more about my family's secret past. Yes, I've considered that she might be dangerous, especially considering the great lengths old grandpa went to get my mother away from her.

But I'm pretty sure I can handle a confrontation with an octogenarian, no matter how intimidating she may be.

Anyway, I tell you all this now because the seagulls have finally located my secret grandmother just outside of Katahdin.

And I'm preparing to go meet her for the first time ever. I'm so excited, I can hardly—

Deep breaths.

Okay, I'm scared out of my mind, but that doesn't mean I'm going to pass up this opportunity. I mean, it's like pulling off a bandage, right? I just have to do it if I ever expect the wound beneath to heal.

I stumbled into the kitchen, practically tripping over my oversized slippers as I moved from the hardwood of the dining room to the tile in the kitchen.

"Good morning," Nan sang, floating over and pushing a banana-nut muffin into my hand. "I'll put the coffee on now."

"Thanks," I murmured, shoving the muffin in the general direction of my mouth, and hoping it would end up in the right place. I'd never been a morning person. Even less so since developing my fear of electric coffee makers.

Don't judge. I'm sure if you ever got electrocuted, you'd fear the appliance that attacked you, too.

I'd tried a million different caffeine solutions from canned coffee to instant powder, and most recently a French press. Nothing beat the freshly brewed stuff, though. It was the whole experience, really. The smell, the sound, all of it.

Thankfully, Nan was only too happy to aid in my addiction.

And so I munched on my baked good while she tidied up the kitchen and the coffee brewed. When it finished, Nan poured me a cup and mixed a bit of pumpkin spice flavored creamer in. It was one of her greatest joys to discover PSL off season, which meant it was always in season for me.

She allowed me to take a few life-giving sips before attempting a conversation. Smart woman.

"What have you got planned for today, dear?" she asked, pouring a cup for herself, and then drifting toward the living room.

I dutifully followed, shuffling my feet so that the little kitty heads on my slippers shook with each motion. Nan had purchased them for me as a Valentine's gift, remarking how much the plush felines looked like Octo-Cat. I now wore them most days, partially because it made Nan happy and partially because it bugged my cat to no end.

"I should get slippers with little human heads attached. See how you like it," the tabby muttered from atop the sofa, his tail flicking in tell-tale irritation.

I took a seat in my favorite armchair while Nan settled herself on the couch. Paisley hopped up beside her and shoved her wet little puppy nose into Octo-Cat's rear end.

"Ick!" he shouted as the hair on his back went up. "Why must you always sniff me there? Surely, the scent hasn't changed from yesterday!"

"Good morning, big brother!" the little dog squealed. She wagged her tail so hard, her whole body shook from the effort.

Octo-Cat growled and ran away to hide.

And so went our morning routine.

"Dear?" Nan prompted, casting a quizzical glance my way. "Your plans for today?"

Oh! Oh, right.

"Sorry. The pets were distracting me," I mumbled to buy myself some time. Now that I had enough caffeine in my system to form a few coherent thoughts, I realized what I needed to do, and it was the very thing I'd been dreading all night. No wonder I was so tired this morning.

"Nan?" I asked, fixing my eyes on the mug in my hands as I continued. "Bravo visited last night. He's found my bio grandmother."

"Oh," she said simply.

When I glanced up again, she had her gaze fixed on an indeterminable point in the distance and sat stroking Paisley without really seeing her—or me.

"Nan?" I prompted again. I hated that she felt this way, but I also couldn't live with myself if I didn't at least try to meet the woman who had birthed my mother. Whether she'd been part of our lives or not, she was still an important part of who my mother and I had become.

Nan sighed gently. "I suppose you'll want to go meet her, then."

"Yes," I answered firmly. That was not up for debate, no matter how much Nan disliked the idea. But I had a plan to soften the blow...

I waited for her eyes to meet mine, and then I flashed her a reassuring smile. "I want you to come with me."

2

an traced her finger along the rim of her mug, then winced. "Oh, shoot. I can't. I already have something planned for that day."

I cleared my throat. "Um, I haven't said what day I'm planning to go yet."

She hit herself in the forehead with her palm, and a few drops of coffee sloshed out onto her neon pink yoga pants. "Silly me!" she cried. "I better go treat this stain before it sets." She rushed into the kitchen far faster than she normally moved around the house.

When I joined her there, she was manically dabbing at her lap with a wet paper towel.

"Nan, we need to talk about this," I said gently.

"It's not coming out. I'm going to throw these in the wash," she muttered, then rushed past me, heading straight for the stairs.

I sighed and trudged up the stairs after her. "Come with me to meet her," I called through her closed bedroom door. "Please. I want you there."

She didn't say anything for several moments. Just as I decided she wasn't going to answer me at all, the door creaked open, and Nan's fingers wrapped around the edge.

One wide eye looked out at me through the tiny opening. "You don't understand, dear. That other woman—your true grandmother—she must hate me for what I did."

"You didn't do anything," I insisted, trying and failing to pull the door open wider. "My grandfather was the one who took Mom away. He forced your hand."

"And I chose to keep you both hidden, even when she came looking all those years later." She let out a shaky breath and cast her eyes to the floor. "If I were her, I'd hate me."

"Don't talk like that. Mom and I have both had great lives, thanks in large part to you." I smiled wide, meaning each word with everything I had. "Plus, doesn't time heal all wounds?"

She shook her head slowly on the other side of the door. I could just barely discern the motion. "Live long enough, and you'll learn that's not true," she muttered eerily.

"But Nan," I whined, not knowing what else I could say to make this better. I'd waited for months after finding out I had a secret grandmother—months for any clues to turn up and even more for the seagulls to locate her. I couldn't just *not* meet her. But I also hated to see Nan hurting like this.

"Please don't ask me again," she whispered. "You know I have a hard time saying no to you."

"But I can't do this on my own," I insisted, not trying to burden her but rather to show how important she was to me—to this.

We both sighed.

"Then take Charles with you, or your mother for that matter," Nan said before pressing the door shut between us.

The sound of overgrown claws scrabbled across the hardwood floor, then stopped.

"Mommy," a small voice rose from beside me.

I glanced down to find Paisley staring up at me with a slowly wagging tail.

"I'll go with you," she volunteered before tucking her tail over her privates and dipping her head. "But I don't think you should ask Nan again. She doesn't like it."

I sighed. Leave it to a dog to be more perceptive than me. "You're right." I bent down to scoop Paisley into my arms.

She immediately began to lick my face and make happy high-pitched noises. "I love you, Mommy."

"I love you, too."

Technically, Paisley was Nan's dog, but that didn't stop her from calling me *Mommy*. It worked, considering everyone in town called my grand-mother Nan, even those who weren't related. Also, I was the only human who could understand her, and Paisley loved shouting the maternal moniker whenever she got a chance.

Her first family had abandoned her to the animal shelter, so I think she needed the added reassurance that when she called out for her family, someone answered back in kind.

I carried Paisley with us as I headed back downstairs. Nan clearly needed some time to herself to process everything, but I needed someone to talk it over with.

Mom was out of the question. Yes, it was *her* birth mother I was planning to go meet, but I wanted to make sure our missing family member was receptive to us before involving Mom. It would be a much bigger blow to her—should this other woman reject us—than it would be to me. Although that would be a sting I'd have a hard time recovering from as well. Still, I loved my mom, and I wanted to protect her if I could.

Yes, my missing grandmother had tried to approach Nan years ago, but who was to say that time hadn't hardened her heart to us?

There were so many unknowns in this situation, and no one I could turn to for advice, either. Because nobody else had gone through a situation like this before—at least not anyone I knew. And the last thing I wanted to do was entrust such a doozy of a family drama to strangers on an Internet message board or social media site.

I didn't want to bother Charles at work, especially since he'd just taken the long weekend off and this was his first day back at the office. I decided to shoot him a quick text: *Call me when you get a break at work. No rush.*

Much to my surprise, my phone began ringing almost immediately after I hit send.

"What's up?" Charles asked when I picked up the call.

"Oh, hey. I didn't mean that you needed to call right away," I chided him. "You need to focus on your work. At least that's what you're always telling me."

He chuckled at my attempt to scold him. I normally never gave him guff like this, but I'd also been hoping for some more time to sort my thoughts out for myself before attempting to share them with him.

"Yeah, but it will be good to have a quick break before switching client files," he said. "Long day ahead. Probably a long night, too."

"I'm sorry," I apologized without knowing why.

"Nothing to be sorry for. This is what I signed up for when I became a lawyer. And you know I love it. Also, I love you..." He paused dramatically, and I could just picture the big goofy grin that accompanied this silence. *"Fiancée."*

A tiny thrill rushed through me. "I love you, too, *fiancé.*"

His smile came through in his words, and I was pretty sure it matched mine. "Now this time really tell me. What's up?"

"Bravo found my grandmother," I revealed, then pressed my lips into a tight line.

Charles sucked air in through his teeth. "Never a dull moment, huh?"

I smiled and shook my head even though he couldn't see the gesture. Talking to him was just natural like that. It never felt like there was any distance between us when we chatted about our days. "Nope."

"So when are we going to meet her? I am invited, right?"

I let out a giant sigh of relief. "Yes, please come with me," I said so fast all my words ran into each other.

"Darling, you couldn't keep me away. I want to be there for my fiancée whenever and however I can. By the way, you're my fiancée."

I smiled to myself. Oh, how I wished I could give him a giant hug of gratitude just then. "I love you, fiancé," I said, twirling my hair like a giggling schoolgirl.

"Uh-oh," Charles said and then let out a rolling groan. "Just got an urgent email. Gotta go, but I'll call you when I take lunch. I can't wait to hear all the sordid details. Bye. Love you."

Well, there was a pretty major thing decided at

least. I probably should have asked Charles first, considering I'd just agreed to be his partner in life. It was hard to break nearly thirty years of seeing Nan as my main partner and confidant, but I guess that was part of growing up. Growing. Changing.

I just hoped things wouldn't change too much.

3

I spent the rest of that week trying on various outfits and attempting a cool new style with my hair. I'd only get one chance to make a first impression on my grandmother, and I really wanted her to like me.

It was silly, but a small part of me thought that if I nailed my outward appearance, I could tip the scales in my favor. After all, I knew next to nothing about this woman. Only that the grandpa I hadn't known deemed her an unfit mother decades ago, and that the seagulls had hinted she might have strange abilities like mine. But how would I even be able to determine that? It's not like I could come right out and ask her such a bizarre question. All that hard work I was doing to look good would go —*whoosh*—right down the drain.

As it turned out, Charles had a busy week at work but was putting in early mornings and long nights at the office so he could leave a couple hours early on Friday. Together, we would head to Katahdin and this cute little bed-and-breakfast we had decided to book based on the online reviews.

Nan made a full-time job of avoiding me. Rather than joining me for morning coffee, she'd brew a pot and leave it on the counter so that I could heat it up in the microwave myself. Each day she had a different reason for being gone, but I knew they were all excuses.

I couldn't wait to punctuate this chapter of our lives with a big, fat period. We both needed to meet my missing grandmother and be done with it. The unknown that would come from this relationship had lingered over our heads for far too long.

With no new P.I. cases coming my way and every possible combination of clothing exhausted, I was quickly running out of ways to keep my hands and mind occupied. I attempted to lose myself in my favorite book series. But my brain was too busy with all its myriad questions to focus on the words before me.

I checked social media, even my long since defunct MySpace account. Yes, I was that desperate for ways to keep myself busy.

I just wanted to get this whole thing over with, but I also knew I wasn't strong enough to go on this crazy adventure by myself.

It was at that point a most excellent thought occurred to me. I could enlist the help of someone else to research my grandmother while I waited for my chance to go meet her in person. I had this thought on Wednesday—two days before Charles and I were scheduled to leave and three days before we'd actually get the chance to meet my grand-mother, provided everything went well.

I had to do something to pass the long, anguish-filled hours, or I'd have found my grandmother but lost my mind.

Which brought me back to my would-be helper. She traveled a lot, but she was also the only person I knew with ties to the Katahdin area. And so I gave Sharon a call.

Sharon and her cat Chessy traveled up and down the coast in a luxury RV funded by their upcoming reality show. The cat was the real apple of the producer's eye, but he and his human came as a package deal.

When I first met Sharon at the RV park just last weekend, I'd mistakenly assumed she was a killer. Hey, sometimes that happened in my line of work.

Once I figured out that she was just a busybody without a single mean bone in said body, I actually grew to like her a lot. She'd been kind and welcoming to Charles, Octo-Cat, and me when no one else at the campsite had taken any efforts to get to know us. That made her good people in my book.

Also, busybodies and private investigators were pretty much a match made in heaven. True, I needed her insights on a personal matter, but that just made me all the more eager to recruit her to my cause.

Sharon picked up on the fourth ring. "Hello? Hello! Are you still there?" she shouted into the phone. "Oh, please don't tell me I'm too late! I just had to finish up in the bathroom, and— "

"Sharon," I interrupted, having to shout so she could hear me. "It's me, Angie. Do you remember meeting me last weekend?"

"Angie Russo, mother to one Octo-Cat and girl-friend to one of the most handsome fellas I've ever seen in all my life. Yes, hello, Angie. What can I do for you?"

"Actually, Charles and I are engaged now," I said as a delicious smile spread across my face.

Sharon crooned happily at this news and then started recounting every wedding she'd ever attended.

I had to interrupt her again. "Yes, yes, we're both very excited, and you'll definitely receive an invite, but that's not why I called."

She sucked in a deep breath and then let out a long, belabored "Ohhh?"

"Well, it's a long story," I admitted.

"Do go on." I could practically see her grabbing a snack and settling in at her RV's booth seat. "Long stories are my favorite kind."

And so I told her everything, leaving out any part that included talking animals, which was no small feat, let me tell you.

"So that's why I'm calling," I said after pausing only briefly so as not to invite any wild conversational tangents from her end. "To see if you can help me find out some info about my grandmother before I come out to meet her this weekend."

"Now who's this Bravo fella again? And why isn't he helping to fill in these details, seeing as he's the one who found her for you?"

"Just an old friend from... uh, Charles's time in

the service." Well, that was almost true, except Charles's service was to a militarized flock of seagulls rather than an actual government body. "He had to fly out of town for a bit, but I'm wondering if you're still in Katahdin, maybe you could—?"

This time Sharon was the one to interrupt. "Darling, you just leave it to me. Tell me her name and whatever info you have, and I'll fill in the rest."

"Oh, so you are still there? Good!"

"No, but I'm turning this RV around and heading that way right now."

I loved this woman. Seriously, how had I ever seen her as anything but a friend? "Her name is Marilyn Jones," I said, picturing the old birth certificate Pringle had unearthed from the attic. "She's in her eighties and lived in Larkhaven, Georgia, at one point, but I don't know much more than that."

"You will," Sharon promised. "Just give me forty-eight hours."

"Perfect, because that's just about as much time as we have."

"You'll let me pay you a visit once you've checked in at Katahdin, won't you?"

"Sharon, thank you. Thank you so, so much."

"Don't fret it, honey. That's what friends are for. Plus, Chessy and I always did love a good mystery."

It was at this point I realized Sharon was basically me minus the boyfriend and plus a decade or two.

Honestly, I kind of loved that.

4

That Friday, I was like a kid at Christmas waiting for Santa. I couldn't eat. I couldn't sleep. I just sat on the living room couch, watching for Charles.

I knew he would pick me up between two and three so we could make it to the Katahdin area before rush-hour traffic hit, but I still planted myself on that couch as soon as I cracked an eye open after one very restless night of failed sleep.

Sharon and I played phone tag most of that morning. I was always it, trying to catch her. Even though she wasn't that old, she hated texting—said it took away that human connection society so desperately craved. Yeah, it's not what I would have expected to hear from an up-and-coming reality star, either.

She'd managed to unearth some info about my long-lost grandmother Marilyn Jones but was being coy about it. If conversations were meant for the phone, she reasoned, important ones should be had face-to-face. And no matter how hard I tried, I couldn't get her to reveal her findings otherwise. This meant our calls were solely about finalizing our plans for meeting up.

Once that was taken care of at last, I was left waiting for Charles with only Paisley at my side to stick it out. Nan, of course, had disappeared, as was becoming normal for her these days. Octo-Cat complained that he had not enjoyed his nightly feline excursions because of how restless I'd been. Apparently, whatever he did at night was completely ruined by the very thought of me blearily stumbling upon his antics. I didn't want to touch that one with a ten-foot cat toy, quite frankly.

"Is it time yet?" Paisley ruffed, hopping off my lap and pressing her paws into the back of the loveseat to peer out the window; her little tail beat furiously.

"Not yet," I said with a moan. This was at least the hundredth time she'd asked me that day, and every time I had to tell her 'not yet,' her ears fell back against her head and she let out a sad whine.

"Oh," she squeaked before sinking back onto the couch and curling into a tiny, shivering ball. As much as I hated to wait, I hated seeing her like this even more.

"I've got an idea," I said, putting on the happiest voice I could manage, given the current circumstances.

Her deer-shaped Chihuahua head popped up, over-sized triangle ears erect once again as she tilted her muzzle to the side.

"Let's play fetch," I said as I slapped my palms against my lap to make this declaration even more irresistible and exciting.

Paisley flew off the couch in an impressive display of athleticism, then slid across the hardwood floor until she found the small stash of toys she liked to keep tucked away. She pranced back over with a tiny stuffed lamb clenched proudly between her teeth.

"Good girl," I enthused. Octo-Cat hated being talked to like a baby or a pet, but Paisley lapped it right up.

She dropped the toy at my feet and began to

kick her legs back in excitement, my sweet little chicken.

I picked up the toy, faked throwing it once or twice, and then launched it across the room.

Paisley scampered after it, barking the whole way.

I waited.

And waited.

When she didn't return after a full minute had passed, I got up to check on her...

And found Octo-Cat nestled on top of her hoard of toys with the little lamb clutched between his paws, claws extended and pressed right into the soft fleece.

"Why?" I demanded, thrusting a hand on my hip.

"You're anxious, which makes her anxious, which makes me anxious. It's a whole vicious cycle," the tabby said around a yawn. He let out a low growl as he so often liked to do when he was feeling testy, which was almost all the time. "I'm ending it here."

"No, you're only making things worse," I countered, reaching down to snag Paisley's toy from him.

Octo-Cat growled again and batted my hand

away. He didn't even bother to retract his claws first.

Paisley began to bark and kick back her feet again. Unlike Octo-Cat, who always had something to say, Paisley sometimes stuck to the pure guttural sounds of barking, whining, and woofing—no added context necessary.

"Ouch," I cried, ripping my hand away. "Why do you have to be so mean?"

"It's for your own good," he answered, eyes narrowed and tail flicking. That thing was like a metronome, steadily counting the beats until his next tantrum.

I narrowed my eyes right back at him and crossed my arms over my chest. "No, it's not."

"Fine, whatever." He sighed mightily, as if this very conversation were miles beneath him. "It just makes life more interesting, you know?"

I rolled my eyes. Why could he never give me a day off from his signature snark? And it was even worse when he admitted that he bugged me simply for entertainment's sake.

"Well, I don't exactly need your help with that," I muttered through clenched teeth.

"Because waiting by the window for Prince Charming to ride up on that white horse and rescue you from your boredom is oh-so riveting?" Octo-Cat shook his head then sneezed.

"I knew I shouldn't have let you subscribe to Disney+," I shouted in a huff.

He let out a laugh worthy of a classic animated villain but refused to relent.

"Sorry, Paize," I said at last, drifting away from the bad kitty and taking up my seat by the window once more.

Did my cat have a point? *Yes.*

Would I ever admit that to him? *Oh, heck no!*

Doing so would only make his sizable head even bigger. That cat was already vain enough without any added assistance from me.

"I'm coming, by the way," the feline bully informed me once Paisley had finally stopped barking at him and come to settle on my lap. He walked over, placing one foot carefully in front of the other, tail and nose both held high. I imagined him on a tight rope in the jungle with angry crocs snapping underneath, but that only made me feel marginally better.

"Who says you're coming?" I demanded,

blinking hard to clear my eyes of the imaginary crocs.

"I do, and as you know, I'm the highest authority on this and all other matters." He jumped up onto the coffee table and sat before me, padding at the polished wood as if it were a warm blanket.

"Why do you even want to come? Remember how you used to hate the car? What happened to that?"

"What can I say? I'm evolving. It's possible for some, though not for others." He shot a sideways glance at Paisley and sneered. Sometimes I really questioned his love for her, but he liked the little pound puppy as much as he could like anyone, I guessed.

I waited for him to go on rather than pointing out the slight to Paisley. It would only hurt her feelings.

He sighed when I didn't take the bait. "Okay, maybe Pringle got me somewhat invested in his reality TV programming."

"So you're going because you want to see Sharon and Chessy again?" He'd hated meeting them both last weekend, so this made zero sense to me.

Octo-Cat made a terrible noise like he was about to barf on the carpet.

And then he actually did it.

"Eww, gross!" I cried. "What is wrong with you?"

He chuckled. "Oh, it's not about what's wrong with me. This time it's about that whole messed up family dynamic you have going on, and I refuse to miss out on the big reveal."

"So glad I have your support," I mumbled, then went to get a roll of paper towels to take care of his mess.

If there was one thing my cat excelled at, it was adding the occasional injury to the steady stream of insults that worked their way off that sandpaper tongue.

Sometimes I really wished he would find a hobby.

5

"So how did you find this place again?" I asked Charles as we rolled up to a small bed-and-breakfast that sat near the shores of a beautiful lake. We'd elected to stay a short way out of Katahdin proper because Charles and I both liked it best when we were near the water—him being a California boy, me a Maine girl.

"One of the associates at work told me about this site that only lists hotels and rentals where pets are allowed," he explained as he pulled to a stop in the small gravel parking lot out front. "I filtered by waterfront properties, and this was the closest property with a vacancy. It also had decent reviews, so I figured why not?"

"Decent, huh?" I asked, raising one eyebrow in extreme suspicion.

"Yeah, but don't read too much into that. You know how online reviews can be." He paused for a moment, regarding me carefully. "Not everything is a mystery just waiting to be solved."

"Says you," I shot back as I unbuckled my seatbelt and clambered out of the car. I held the door open so that Paisley and Octo-Cat could hop out, too.

"I love it here!" Paisley cried and then took off running in wide, looping circles. "Wheeeee!"

"Why did we bring her again?" Octo-Cat demanded of me with a sneer.

I didn't get a chance to answer, though, because Paisley zipped and zoomed out of view. I was just about to call her back when a sharp yelp rent the air. We all took off running in pursuit of the sound.

Octo-Cat moved the fastest out of the three of us, which meant he was first on the scene. I couldn't see anything, but I heard a mighty hiss followed by a low, ominous growl. When I finally rounded the corner, I found my tabby in a beach stand-off with an enormous orange Persian.

Paisley cowered behind Octo-Cat, shaking violently as the two cats stared each other down.

"Nobody hurts my kid sister," Octo-Cat hissed at the strange feline.

The orange Persian extended his claws and took a swipe at Octo's face.

"You s-st-struck me?" he sputtered in shock. "You actually struck me?"

The Persian wore a satisfied expression on his flat face. "Maybe next time you'll remember who lives here and who's simply an unwelcome intruder," he said, then raised his tail high and sauntered off down the sandy beach.

"That does it! I'll end him! I'll— "

I grabbed Octo-Cat in my arms before the fight could escalate any further. The last thing we needed was to get kicked out of our accommodation before I even had a chance to meet my grandma.

"Be the bigger person," I said through gritted teeth.

"There's so much wrong with that statement I don't even know where to begin," my cat shot back. "Just keep that giant, fluffy wad of mouse breath away from me."

Funny how much he hated this cat with its long hair and flat face, when his true love Grizabella was a former show Himalayan and looked quite similar if you ignored the coloration. I guessed that meant my cat wasn't a breedist, and that was a good thing for sure.

"I'm sorry, Mommy," Paisley ground out, coming to stand at my feet. "I was just so happy to be out of the car."

"It's fine. It's not either of your faults. Just calm down and try to put it out of your mind," I cooed.

Charles grabbed Paisley and clutched her against his chest. "Everything okay?" he said, expression askance.

"It will be," I assured them all. "It's just been a long week for all of us."

"So we're staying?" Charles wanted to confirm.

"We're staying," I said with a tight nod, then motioned for everyone to head back the way we'd come. "Let's go check in to our room. Sharon will be here soon, and I want some time to get ourselves set up first."

Charles and I entered the sprawling ranch, each carrying an agitated pet in our arms. Just past the door, we found an elderly woman with dyed orange hair that matched the mean Persian cat's to the exact shade.

"I've been expecting you," she said, uncrossing her legs and placing the paperback novel she'd been reading face-down on the arm of her chair. "Mr. and Mrs. Longfellow, I presume?"

I smiled at that. It was the first time I'd ever heard it aloud, and I rather liked the sound.

"Almost," Charles said with a huge grin to match mine. "For now, it's Mr. Longfellow and Ms. Russo."

"I see," the woman said, tightening her expression. She drifted over to a desk at the corner of the room. "I'll just update your reservation from a king to two doubles then. That's an easy enough fix."

Charles looked like he wanted to say something, but I nudged him in the side and shook my head. Separate beds would make the sleeping situation with the pets much easier anyway, since Octo-Cat threw a right proper fit whenever Paisley tried to snuggle up to him.

"My name is Millicent Strobel," the woman droned, handing us the keys to our room. "I can normally be found here in the front room if you need anything. We don't have room service, but I do serve breakfast from five thirty until eight o'clock."

Wow, that was early, but I doubted I'd be able to sleep well tonight, anyway.

My guess was that the B and B lady gave this

same spiel to all her guests, considering the dry, bored way she addressed us.

"Thank you, Millie," I said when it became clear Millicent expected us to say something in response.

"No," she corrected harshly, taking the opportunity to look us both up and down and shaking her head in apparent disappointment. "Don't do that. It's Millicent to you. Or better yet, Mrs. Strobel. Now if you don't mind."

I said nothing as she resettled herself in the chair and returned to her book.

With that dismissal, we left her behind as quickly as possible—for one, because she obviously was done with us, but also because Octo-Cat had begun to weigh heavily in my arms.

"Well, I think we solved the mystery of the reviews." Charles set Paisley on the floor so he could wrestle the doorknob with both hands. "I think it's stu—Oh, there it goes," he said when the door finally popped out.

"Jeez. For a minute there, I thought this was her way of getting rid of us."

Octo-Cat sniffed hesitantly around the room, his tail almost a bristle brush of aggravation. "I wish she would've," he snarked. "This place smells awful."

"Hush, you," I admonished with a scowl.

"Whatever," my spoiled kitty shot back. "This one will be my bed." He hopped up on the bed farthest the door and promptly laid out, stretching so as to take up as much of the mattress as possible.

I rolled my eyes, but he was too busy enjoying the soft bed to notice.

"Can I go out?" Paisley asked, scratching at the doorframe.

"Stay close," I warned before sliding open the glass door that led out to the beautifully manicured property. "You don't want to run into that mean kitty again."

"Yes, Mommy! I will, Mommy!" she called before taking off at full speed once more.

Charles took me in his arms. "Alone at last," he said, giving me a slow, lingering kiss.

"Kill me now!" Octo-Cat yelled.

Yup, this would definitely not be a romantic weekend. Not unless we got our cat his own room, and I just didn't have that in the budget, unfortunately.

6

"Knock, knock." Sharon's singsong voice floated into our room a short while later. I turned and saw her standing outside the glass sliding door that separated our bedroom from a short walk down to the lake and its sandy beaches.

Charles yanked on the handle to open the door, and I rushed out to give her a big, fat hug. Once we'd given each other a good squeeze, I pulled back and studied her face for any hints as to what she'd learned about my missing grandmother.

She simply raised a finger and shook it at me. "First let's get this picnic situated, and then we can dish."

I followed her eyes toward a nearby pair of

Adirondack chairs with a small wooden plank table nestled between them. On the table sat a beautiful wicker picnic basket. When Sharon said she'd be bringing dinner, I had assumed she'd pick up a pizza or something easy. I hoped she hadn't gone to too much trouble, considering I'd already called in a huge favor from her, and our acquaintanceship was hardly even a week old.

"Oh, don't you worry," she said as if reading my mind. "It's just my newly famous lobster rolls and bisque. I'm staying away from desserts of all sorts after what happened to our poor Junetta."

I nodded stoically. It wasn't Sharon's fault that someone else had placed poison in her pie, but clearly the affront had taken a toll on her all the same.

"Lobster rolls!" Octo-Cat cried before zipping through the door. "No way I'm missing this!"

Paisley came surging forward from places unknown to chase after him.

"So just a light meal then," Charles quipped as he closed up our room and then plucked the basket from the table.

"Oh, you!" Sharon trilled and hit him playfully on the chest. She wasn't kidding about her attraction to him. Thankfully, I didn't feel even the slightest bit jealous. I knew Charles's heart—and his future—were all mine.

The three of us walked down to the beach, both animals circling back to follow close at our heels.

"Where's Chessy?" I asked, remembering how inseparable Sharon had been from her fluffy white cat when last we met.

"He's staying back in the RV. I just could not get him to agree to the harness today, and he's not well-behaved like your Octavius. He'd run away in a heartbeat if he could. That little man of mine has an adventurer's heart, let me tell you." When Sharon chuckled, her billowing duster cardigan and loosely wrapped pashmina twirled around her hips and thighs.

"Well, at least one cat around here has some sense," Octo-Cat muttered, presumably referring to that Persian from earlier.

"Mommy, that mean cat won't bother us again, will he?" Paisley barked.

I shook my head, unable to answer in mixed company. I really liked Sharon, but she was a gossip *and* a future reality star. If she got word of my special abilities, they'd no doubt become front-page news at some national rag before even a full day could pass.

We reached the beach, and Sharon slipped out of her sandals, sighing happily as her painted toes sunk into the sand. "Still a bit early in the season, but, oh, it's nice."

Charles and I followed suit and padded after her with our bare feet as Paisley splashed around in the ebbing surf and Octo-Cat trotted after us from several yards up shore, refusing to get anywhere near the water.

"It's like one giant litter box out here," he mused. "It would be perfect if not for all the water."

We stopped at an old wooden dock with a paddle boat tethered to either side. Sharon traipsed to the very end and then sat with her legs dangling toward the water.

"I hope you don't mind, I made some supper for the critters, too." She opened up the basket and handed me a lobster roll wrapped snugly in wax paper.

"Oh, yeah." Octo-Cat quivered, his eyes growing comically wide. "Come to papa, you delicious little thing."

I opened the savory-smelling package and set it on the dock in front of him, but Sharon reached over me and scooped it away before my gluttonous cat could manage so much as a single sniff.

"Almost lost your sandwich there!" she said breathlessly, then dipped her hand into the basket and pulled out a much smaller parcel. "*This* is for Octavius."

I popped the lid off the small Tupperware container and set it down beside me, trying to keep my expression neutral.

"What fresh torment is this?" he snarled and stared daggers at both me and Sharon.

Paisley skipped over and stuck her snout in the mush Sharon had prepared for Octo-Cat. It appeared to be canned cat food slathered on a special type of cracker.

"Seafood medley on my own special snack biscuit recipe. Chessy loves it."

"Chessy doesn't have a choice, but I do." Octo-Cat lunged at Sharon, causing her to drop the lobster roll she'd just narrowly saved from him before.

He grabbed it between those sharp, greedy teeth of his and took off running. Paisley used that opportunity to gulp down the specialty cat sandwich. Charles laughed, while Sharon looked like she was going to cry.

"It's okay," I said softly. "I'm much more of a bisque girl myself. I can't wait to try yours."

And with that, her eyes grew bright again. She talked me and Charles through the process of developing her new recipe as she ladled out a serving for each of us.

I listened to every single word, taking slow, contemplative spoonfuls into my mouth. The soup was rich and creamy, filling my stomach perfectly without the help of an added course.

I was grateful for the hot meal but had a hard time following the conversation when there was only one topic I wanted to discuss with Sharon.

When she finally paused to take a bite of her own meal, I saw my chance to get us back to the reason we'd all gathered there that night.

"So about my grandmother..." I started, then bit my lip and waited.

7

Sharon cleared her throat as she wrapped up her uneaten lobster roll and placed it back into the picnic basket. "Oh, sorry. Did you want this?" she offered with an uncharacteristic flush on her cheeks.

"Is it really that bad?" I choked out. Suddenly my chest felt heavy with the weight of an unknown shame. I'd asked for Sharon's help because I was bursting with curiosity—not because I actually expected her to find something terrible about my missing family member.

Charles scooted along the dock until our hips were touching and then wrapped an arm around my shoulders. "I'm sure it's nothing too big," he reassured me.

Sharon cleared her throat again. "Wellllll." She twisted her hands in her lap and refused to meet my eye, instead gazing out across the lake as the gentle ripples reflected the sunlight.

"Please just tell me," I begged. My stomach threatened to give up the bisque that I'd just filled it with. "I need to know," I added softly. "Please don't make me wait any longer."

Sharon nodded; a tuft of her short blonde hair caught the breeze and flickered distractingly. "It took me a while to find out much of anything. She's changed her name, you see."

"Oh, so she remarried?" Charles asked brightly, drumming his fingers against my upper arm. "I mean, that's probably to be expected seeing as it's been about sixty years."

"Her first name," Sharon corrected.

At the same time, I said, "She and my grand-dad were never married. He was a McAllister. She was a Jones."

"She still is a Jones," Sharon murmured. "She was born Marilyn. Then went by Mary for a spell, and now she's Lyn."

"So she switched up her nickname? A lot of people do that, right?" Charles reasoned, always so optimistic. I honestly didn't know how he did it.

"Actually, she switched up her legal name. It took some digging to find all those iterations belonged to the same person." She paused and drew in several deep breaths.

What was coming next? I almost couldn't stand the anticipation, no matter how brief my wait.

"Luckily—or perhaps unluckily," Sharon continued with a sigh, "she was in the papers a lot, your grandmother."

Charles tensed at my side, tightening his grip on my shoulder. "Why?"

"She's lived a troubled life," Sharon said with a grimace. "She's done a few rounds in prison. A few in the psychiatric ward. Seems to be a bit of a bad egg."

I stumbled to my feet. Perhaps Sharon wasn't the friend I'd thought she was. That was my fault for trusting a near stranger with something so important.

"What? Why? Why would you say that?" I demanded, feeling outraged on behalf of a woman I'd never even met. Sharon was saying my grand-mother was a bad egg, and well, we were from the same nest.

"I don't know. The records are sealed, but I

could see she got picked up once every few years. Did small amounts of time in prison, until suddenly they started sending her to the asylum instead."

"Not guilty by way of insanity," Charles murmured.

"Also, it's not called that anymore," I added spitefully.

"Sorry, I guess I'm a bit old-fashioned, and I know that's not always a good thing. I don't mean to make you feel bad, hunny bunny," Sharon said, softening my reaction to her harsh choice of words. But then she said, "I don't think you're crazy, even if your grandmother is."

I turned toward Charles with wide eyes. "Do you think she's dangerous? Is that why my grandfather kidnapped his own child? To keep my mom safe?"

He shook his head slowly but didn't glance up to meet my gaze. "I wish I had the answers for you, but there's only one person we can really ask."

"I found her number," Sharon said, pulling out a business card that she'd kept tucked in her jeans pocket. It had Sharon's info on one side and another number scrawled with a failing ink pen on the back. She handed the card to me, and I read the string of numbers over again and again. I didn't recognize the area code, suggesting she probably moved around a fair bit, too—or had at least moved somewhat recently, even before she'd arrived in Maine.

That checked out, since the seagulls had eyes on her in the Blueberry Bay area but then lost her temporarily when she moved to Katahdin.

Just where had she lived before? And how many different places had she ended up over the years? I knew she'd lived in Larkhaven, Georgia, when my mom was born and caught up with Nan in New York when Mom was a pre-teen. But where else had she journeyed these long years apart?

"It's a California area code," Charles informed us. "A couple counties over from where I grew up."

"I wonder when she lived there," I said, turning the card over in my hand with a frown. There was so much I didn't know about this person—this stranger. Even though we shared some DNA, I knew absolutely nothing about her. Was I crazy for pursuing this?

"Are you going to call her?" Sharon prompted, nodding toward my hands.

I took a deep breath, then nodded slowly. Yes, maybe I was a little nuts, but I'd never considered that a bad thing before. "I've come this far. No sense in giving up now."

I misdialed twice before I finally got it right, and then the phone rang twice, three times... seven, eight. Nobody answered, not even the voicemail service.

"Now what?" I asked Charles as tears threatened to spill. I kept pumping myself up, only to be let down. All that adrenaline coursing through my veins didn't just go away. I stayed keyed up for hours after each near encounter with my grandmother. I had to meet her—and soon—for my own sanity.

"Don't worry. We'll find her," he promised.

"I'm sorry I couldn't be of more help," Sharon said gently as she struggled to her feet and opened her arms to invite a hug. "I really wanted to have good news to give you."

"It's okay," I said, hugging her once more. I couldn't be mad at her. Not about this. Not about anything, really. It was just so hard to keep my emotions straight given how many highs and lows I'd experienced lately. I needed...

I wasn't sure what I needed, but I had to figure that one out for myself.

"I appreciate the help," I told Sharon, then

turned to look at Charles as well, "but if it's all right with you, I think I need some time to sit alone with my thoughts."

harles and I escorted Sharon to her car before returning to the B and B via the main reception area.

Millicent still sat in that same chair, eyes glued to the pages of her book. I don't even think she noticed us come through—something I was grateful for.

"I know I shouldn't say this, but I can't wait for this whole thing to be over," I murmured to Charles as he fiddled with the lock and key.

"You can say and feel however you want, Ang. It's all perfectly understandable," he assured me with a sad smile, continuing to struggle with the doorknob.

Octo-Cat moaned. "I could open that thing ten times as fast, and I don't even have opposable thumbs." He and Paisley had rejoined us on the walk to the parking lot, and neither seemed any worse for the wear—which probably meant that mean old Persian was off troubling somebody else for the moment.

"Be nice," the little dog yipped. "He's doing the best he can. Right, Mommy?"

"Well, clearly UpChuck's best isn't quite good enough, is it?" came the cat's snide reply.

I pressed my fingers into my temples and rubbed. "Ugh. I thought we'd moved past that horrible nickname."

"What?" Charles asked with a furrowed brow.

"Here. Let me help," I said rather than answering his actual question.

I took over and struggled for a couple moments before finally wresting the lock open. Another couple—old and married from what I could tell—came down the hallway and entered their room with no problem.

"I bet that was the room we were supposed to have," I whispered to Charles. We both rolled our eyes.

The door eased open, catching me by surprise when it finally gave way.

"Took you long enough!" Octo-Cat said, heaving a dramatic sigh as he entered the room. "Seriously, humans. What are they even good for?"

I walked in behind him and was surprised to feel a chilly wind rush past.

"Charles, I thought you closed that." I said, flopping over on the bed nearest the door, since Octo-Cat had made it clear none of us were to mess with *his* bed.

"I thought I had," he said, going over to secure the sliding door once again.

I could hear a soft swish as he flipped the lock latch back and forth. He opened and closed the glass door a few more times before turning back to face me.

"That's odd," he muttered.

"What is?" I asked, sitting up and petting Paisley as she climbed into my lap.

"This latch system doesn't work."

"So the door just slid open on its own?"

He nodded before coming over to join me on the bed. "Seems like it. I guess we can jam something in there to hold it before we go back out again."

"Isn't it kind of weird that one lock works too

well and the other not at all?" I asked, quirking my head to the side.

Charles sunk onto the bed next to me and pulled me into his side. "Not weird. Just a simple coincidence. Now you said you needed some time alone with your thoughts. Did you mean alone together or *alone* alone?"

"Would it be all right if I had just a little bit of time to myself?" I asked with an apologetic grimace. It was strange how I'd been craving his company all week, and now that we were finally together, I needed to ask for space. It was nothing against Charles, of course. But Sharon had dropped a doozy on me. No wonder she hadn't wanted to tell me over the phone.

My fiancé pressed a firm kiss into my hairline. "Tell you what, you get some rest, and I'll head out to see if I can make some sense of Bravo's directions. Can you text those to me again?"

I breathed a happy sigh of relief. "That would be wonderful. Thank you for understanding. I grabbed my phone from the nightstand and brought up the notes app. I'd recorded the seagull's guidance there, and now I copy-pasted it into a fresh text for Charles.

Initially, Bravo had said he would take me to my

grandmother, which I thought meant he'd be joining us for the trip.

Nope.

He actually meant he would take us there with his words. One thing I'd learned in all my conversations with animals is that every single species had a different way of viewing the world. I had the least experience with birds, given their flighty nature, but I figured between me, Charles, and the pets, we'd be able to find our way.

I pushed the button to send my text, and Charles's phone pinged a couple of seconds later.

He cleared his throat, then read aloud. "'Follow the water until the air begins to chill. Stop at the green dumpster with the good fries.' The good fries? What's good to a seagull? Oh, here we go. 'Follow the scent of fish several leagues until you reach a tan building with loose trash can lids. The dogs to the south have been restrained, so eat all you want. Short hops from here through the human encampment. Approach in a zigzag to avoid floodlights and bad air. Cross the dead river and find the target amongst the stick-colored domiciles with pink sentinels standing guard...' Seriously?" he asked with a chuff once he'd gotten to the end. "None of this makes any sense."

"He worked hard on those directions. If I had asked for clarification I would have offended him," I said with a tight-lipped smile. "Anyway, they're from a bird's-eye view. They don't think of things the way we do, so of course they don't describe them that way, either."

"I can't wait to eat the good fries!" Paisley chimed in, making me giggle.

But Charles still appeared quite frazzled. "Is she even in Katahdin at all? Do we know for sure?"

"Bravo said she was, but this isn't anywhere near his flock's territories, so I doubt he knows the actual boundaries."

"Right, so it's a wild goose chase—er, a wild seagull chase—for me. But it'll be fine. I can figure this out. I just have to think like the witness, put myself in his... wings, I guess. I've got this, babe. Enjoy your downtime. Call if you need me, and I'll come straight back."

"Thank you. I love you," I called after him. I really needed this. Of course, I wasn't properly on my own, thanks to the pets.

Octo-Cat had already fallen asleep on the pillow at the head of his bed while Paisley wagged her tail and licked between my fingers. "What now, Mommy?" she asked.

I had to think fast to come up with a valid excuse to be on my own, otherwise her feelings would be deeply hurt. I glanced around the room, landing on the door to the en suite bathroom. "Um, I'm just going to take a nice bubble bath."

"Okay, Mommy! What will I do?" she asked, cocking her head to the side.

"Why don't you curl up and take a nap with Octo-Cat?" I said, picking her up as I stood and then setting her onto the other bed beside the crabby tabby. When he woke up, he was going to be livid. Luckily, I'd already be locked safely away in the next room—provided that lock worked at all. Just to be safe, I crept back into the main room and grabbed my cell phone and bathrobe. That way I'd be prepared if I got stuck and needed to get someone to help me out.

Back in the bedroom, dear, sweet Paisley had wrapped herself around Octo-Cat so that he was the little spoon and she was the big spoon. Never mind that he was more than twice her size. It made for a comical picture, and I snapped a quick photo on my phone before leaving the pets to themselves and retreating to the bathroom to draw my bath.

What an adventure this was shaping up to be already. And no matter how things turned out with my long-lost grandmother, I doubted I'd ever be able to forget even the slightest bit of our journey to find her.

But oh, how I hoped this would end with a happily ever after.

9

Evening gave way to night.

I trusted Sharon and the info she had located on my behalf, but there had to be more to the story. Deep down, I knew my grandmother couldn't be bad. At least that's what I told myself over and over again as I soaked in that clawfoot tub filled past the brim with bubbles.

Eventually, I gave up on relaxing in the bath and tiptoed into the bedroom to try to catch a nap. Cat and dog were both still curled together and snoozing softly, which meant I might actually stand a chance of grabbing some shut-eye. Heavens knew I needed it after the terrible sleep I'd gotten the night before.

I slid off my diamond engagement ring and

placed it on the nightstand beside my phone, then pulled the quilt to my chin and shut my eyes. It didn't take long at all for me to nod off.

I awoke later when Charles returned via the sliding glass door. The room now lay in complete darkness other than the faint glow from his cell phone.

"Sorry, didn't mean to wake you," he whispered as he made his way over to the bed and began to grope for the lamp. "We forgot to jam up the door like we said, and I was having trouble with the lock and key again. Go back to sleep."

"It's okay. I'm up now," I mumbled, helping him with the lamp. Our hands collided, and something went skittering to the hardwood floor below.

"Oops," I said.

Charles dove to the floor so I didn't have to.

I glanced at the empty nightstand just as he popped up with my phone in hand.

"Can you grab my ring, too?" I asked, accepting the cell phone from him.

He returned to his hands and knees and searched under both beds. "Ang, I don't see it down here."

"But it's gotta be there. I took it off before my

nap and put it right by my cell phone," I argued, getting out of bed to help.

We searched for a good five minutes but both came up short. So I decided to ask the cat for help—a decision I did not take lightly, but this was my engagement ring, after all.

"Octo-Cat, have you seen my ring?" I said, right after I picked up Paisley and removed any evidence of their shared nap. He'd never tell me a thing if he discovered what I'd let happen. He had a huge soft spot for the tiny rescue dog, but rarely was it enough to overcome the selfishness that came standard issue with his being an upper-middle-class cat.

"I've seen it," he answered around a yawn. "Nothing special, if you ask me, but then again, neither is UpChuck."

I pulled the pillow out from under him, and he rolled onto the mattress.

"Give that back," he moaned.

"Take what you said back," I demanded.

"No."

"Where's my ring?"

"I don't know."

"Yes, you do. You clearly have it out for Charles, so it makes sense you'd try to sabotage our wedding by—"

"I've had enough," he spat, popping to his feet. "Call me when you come to your senses. C'mon, Mutt."

Paisley looked at me with wide, shimmering eyes.

"Go," I said. "Keep him out of trouble."

She wasted no time scampering after him as Charles crossed the room and opened the sliding door, allowing both animals to disappear into the night.

"It's really not here, is it?" I said, staring hatefully at my bare ring finger. How had I lived with it like this for so long? Darn it, I never should have taken that ring off.

"Let's go check in with reception," Charles suggested, moving toward the wooden door on the other side of our room. At least it was easy to open from the inside. "I saw Millicent was still up when I came through that way."

Sure enough, Millicent sat in her chair with her book. At this point, I had to question whether our proprietress was, indeed, an art installation and not a businesswoman.

"Excuse me?" I said, stopping in front of her.

She held up a finger and continued reading for at least a minute before she finally raised her eyes to meet mine. "Yes?" Her eyes were wide, her expression mostly blank.

"Has anyone turned in a ring for the lost and found?"

"We don't have a lost and found," she replied with no follow-up questions and no hint of apology.

The fluffy orange cat hopped up onto a nearby windowsill to glare at me and Charles. Maybe all my time with Octo-Cat had made me cynical, or maybe I was still miffed about him bullying little Paisley, but something seemed off about him.

"Oh. Well, I have a lost item. A pretty important one at that."

"I'll let you know if anything turns up," Millicent said, tucking an orange curl behind her ear and revealing an earring I hadn't noticed her wearing before—a big dangly one with a little gemmed tassel.

The Persian's eyes zoomed toward the gaudy piece of costume jewelry, and he wiggled his behind as if to attack.

"Not now, Louis," the lady told him. He growled and ran across the room to hide. Poor cat must've been starved for stimulation if he got so worked up over earrings.

"Yeah, well, thanks for your help," I mumbled,

wondering if Millicent would even remember having our conversation.

"Oh, while we have you," Charles interjected, waving his hand in front of her.

Millicent groaned and tore her eyes from the book a second time. "What is it now?"

"There seems to be a problem with the door to our room."

She bobbed her head and shifted her jaw. "Uh-huh. Which one?"

"Both, actually," he said with a chuckle. "One doesn't open, and the other doesn't close."

"Oh, right. I put you in the Shoreline suite. The locksmith should be here early next week to fix both of them. I wasn't going to book anyone in until that was taken care of, but then you two showed up with your little problem, and well, I had to do something to set it right."

Charles's brow furrowed. I could see he was about to go into full-on lawyer mode if I didn't do something fast. "But—"

"Yup! Okay, thanks," I said, grabbing him by the hand and leading him back around outside.

"I don't think she likes us very much," he said once we were both outdoors and out of earshot.

"Who would?" a nasty voice spat.

I looked around and found the big, orange Persian from earlier slinking by. Louis, that was the little scamp's name.

I tamped down my urge to scold him like I would whenever Octo-Cat took up an attitude with me and refocused my attention on Charles.

"Care for a moonlight walk on the beach?" he said, waggling his brows.

"I thought you'd never ask," I said, falling into step beside him as we strolled outside and headed for the water.

"This would have probably been a better proposal than the RV, huh?"

"I liked your proposal," I said, stretching up to give him a quick kiss.

"If you liked that, you'll really like this. I'm pretty sure I found your grandmother."

I gasped. "Really? Where?" It's not that this news surprised me. It just made me so, so happy.

"Oh, no no no," he tsked playfully. "You don't get to jump to the end of the journey after sending me on that seagull chase."

He moved to regale me with tales of his heroic exploits as he tooled all around the Katahdin area, trying to make heads and tails of Bravo's directions. "I may have had to sample a few different fries to help me determine which were the good ones. Well, according to a seagull, anyway."

"Eww, you ate out of the dumpster?"

He fixed me with a wounded expression. "Drive-thru, but thanks for assuming that."

We both laughed for a good long while as we slowly moved along the beach, hand in hand beneath the night sky.

Everything would be okay. I knew it then. I'm pretty sure I'd known it this whole time, but it was easy to forget when my nerves got the best of me.

With Charles at my side, I could conquer anything. We'd meet my grandmother and find my ring.

We just had to take one thing at a time.

One foot in front of the other.

Yes, everything would be just fine.

10

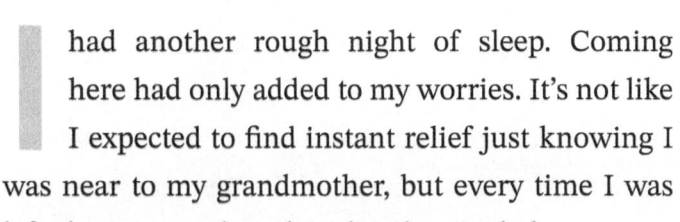

had another rough night of sleep. Coming here had only added to my worries. It's not like I expected to find instant relief just knowing I was near to my grandmother, but every time I was left alone to my thoughts, dread prevailed.

The walk with Charles on the beach had put my mind at ease, but as soon as he drifted to sleep, the swirling cyclone of anxiety wreaked havoc once more.

Sharon's news had set me on edge, and now every new inconvenience—whether big or small—pushed me closer and close to my falling point.

Quarreling animals.

A rude proprietress.

My missing ring.

The unlatchable door.

That last one really irked me. Generally, Maine was a safe place to be, but I didn't like the thought that just anyone could walk off the street and accost us while we were sleeping.

Since I couldn't sleep anyway, I decided to research the bed-and-breakfast online. First I checked the site Charles had used to book our stay, where our host had a 3.5-star average. Some of the less favorable reviews mentioned how rude and off-putting Millicent had been toward them during their stay, but most of the negative remarks centered around far more mundane things—an uncleaned room, cat barf in the hallway, not enough gluten-free breakfast options.

Feeling somewhat justified in my disdain for Mrs. Strobel, I decided to dig deeper, moving on to the more well-known travel sites to see what I could find in the much larger sampling of guest feedback there. One of the more recent reviews actually mentioned the faulty door we'd gotten stuck with. I read on with interest. That was two weeks ago, and still Millicent hadn't bothered to fix the issue. I wondered if she even planned to fix it at all.

How far back did this issue go?

I did a search for "door" within the reviews and found three others that mentioned it. One was written several months ago. It also mentioned an antique brooch that had gone missing. I searched for "missing," "stolen," and other synonyms and found four more reviewers who had lost something valuable while staying in this bed-and-breakfast.

Was Millicent a thief? Were those gaudy earrings I'd noticed earlier taken from an unwitting guest?

And had Millicent moved Charles and me to this room with two double beds not out of judgment but rather to gain access to my engagement ring?

These were the questions on my mind when I finally drifted off.

I didn't stay asleep for long, though. A cold breeze tickled at my cheeks, drawing my eyes to the glass door.

Open again.

Paisley lay curled at my hip, nestled between me and Charles under the blankets, but Octo-Cat's bed sat empty.

I pulled on my robe and worked my feet into my

shoes sans socks, then headed out using my phone as a flashlight.

"Octo-Cat," I whisper-yelled after sliding the door shut after me. It would probably be open again by the time I got back to the room, but that didn't mean I couldn't at least try to close it properly. Had Octavius opened it on his way out, or did someone else enter our room?

I shuddered at the possibility of just that as I moved closer to the lake. An owl hooted in the distance, and a host of crickets sang a song about the night. It was catchy, that ditty of theirs. Perhaps one day I would learn the words for myself.

Right now, I was too worried about my cat to bother with anything else.

A dark shape shifted on the dock, and I increased my pace.

I pulled up short as I spotted Octo-Cat leaping and flipping into the air, almost dancing in the moonlight. This must've been what he was talking about when he mentioned his nighttime activities.

Standing there in the moonlight, I felt a little guilty for intruding on his joy.

"Angela, I can feel you standing there," he said suddenly, falling to all four feet and then pausing on the pier.

"Sorry," I muttered, going over to sit next to him. "I was just having trouble sleeping and you were missing. I got worried."

"I woke up because that stupid door was open again," he said, meticulously grooming himself. "I got up to see what was going on and I spotted that ugly, flat-faced, sorry excuse for a cat wandering around. I was going to give him a piece of my mind, but, of course, he disappeared before I could. You'd figure with a smell like that he'd be easier to follow."

"Don't get into any fights," I warned him.

"Relax, Angela. I know what I'm doing," he purred. "So why couldn't you sleep?"

"The door," I admitted with a sigh.

"Just the door? I figured you'd be nervous about meeting your grandmother," he said, smoothing out his tail. "But you know you don't need to be, right?"

I sat there shocked. Was Octo-Cat actually being... nice? To me? Now?

I stared at him, mouth agape.

"Don't look so surprised. Sometimes your human ways actually make sense," he continued, blinking slowly in my direction. "When we talked about finding my family, I was a bit nervous about the possibility. I mean, how could they possibly be as amazing as I am?"

He chuckled, and I found myself absently petting him behind the ears.

"But I realized something, Angela. If they aren't amazing or awesome, that doesn't change me. Because I'm still a superb specimen of feline perfection, even if they don't quite measure up. I mean, so few could ever hope to hold a candle to this." He postured himself with his chest puffed out and his nose held high, which made me burst out in laughter.

He nodded his approval. "The worst thing that can happen from meeting your grandmother is... well, nothing. Your life doesn't change, and you just go back and live like you always have. And if we're being totally honest here, you have a pretty great life for a human."

I didn't reply. I didn't need to.

If I drew this out, Octo-Cat would just return to his usual snark, and I wanted to savor this moment while I could. And so we sat there in the moonlight for a while longer before heading back to our room.

Yes, I needed the people and animals in my life to help me through this, which at first blush might make me seem weak and incapable of handling my own challenges.

But then again, that's why we have loved ones to begin with. To get us through the bad and to share in the good.

Hopefully tomorrow would bring the latter for Charles, Octo-Cat, Paisley, me...

And my grandmother.

11

The next morning I was already showered, dressed, and ready by the time Charles woke up. I'd spent all week planning my outfit, and now that I was actually wearing it, an odd sense of reverence washed over me.

This was one of the most important things I'd ever done. And whatever happened—good, bad, or somewhere in between—this would be a defining moment of my life.

We fed the pets, then grabbed some coffee from the continental breakfast set-up Millicent had waiting for her guests.

Charles took a pre-packaged Danish, but I was too nervous to even attempt eating anything. Besides, I'd been spoiled by Nan's expert baking all my life and had become something of a muffin snob. The blueberry to cake ratio of the ones sitting before me was all wrong. I didn't have to try them to know that. The baked "goods" also looked more than a few days old. No wonder there had been complaints. The longer we stayed, the more and more reasons I was finding to justify the bad reviews.

"Let me just say it one more time," Charles said as he jabbed his key in the ignition, and I pulled my seatbelt over my lap. "I think I've found the right place, but we won't know for sure until we meet her."

I nodded once. "Right. And I'm going in without any expectations. *Que será será* and all that."

Charles reached for my hand and twined his fingers through mine. "No, you're not. And that's okay. It's okay to want things to go well, so stop giving yourself such a hard time about that. Whatever happens, I'll be right here."

"Holding my hand?" I suggested with a grin.

He returned my smile and gave my hand another squeeze. "If you want me to."

We held hands the entire drive, except for the

few parts where Charles had a left turn to make or we ran into a bit of traffic.

Octo-Cat made occasional retching sounds from the back seat.

Good to see he'd recovered from the strange bout of compassion he'd shown me last night. I wondered if he was always like that at night. If he was only crabby during the day because he was sleepy.

"I can't believe you signed on to be Mrs. UpChuck," my cat ground out, "but then again, the role is perfect for you."

"Thank you," I said with a satisfied grin as the heated leather seat warmed my posterior.

"Huh?" Charles asked, briefly glancing my way.

"Thank you," I repeated, this time to him. "For being here, for being you, for all of this."

"Barf, barf!" Octo-Cat shouted at us.

I ignored him and leaned over to plant a kiss on my fiancé's cheek.

"We're here," Charles announced a short time later, pulling into a condominium complex. "I think."

Every single unit was a dull tan color, both the siding and the roof. It looked like we were stepping into a strange suburban desert right in the middle of Maine.

A group of high schoolers ambled past, their hands pushed down into the pockets of overly baggy jeans. One of them leered at me suggestively, sending a fresh wave of heat to my cheeks.

"Which one is hers?" I asked as Paisley barked furiously at the passers-by.

"Well, this was the one step of the journey I felt confident about. It's the one with all the pink plastic flamingos."

"Oh, right, the pink sentinels," I said, remembering the directions I myself had transcribed. "Do you think she's home?"

Charles turned off the engine and turned his full gaze toward me. "Only one way to find out. You ready?"

I swallowed down the lump that had formed in my throat. It was so thick, it felt as if it were stuck. Suddenly my eyes burned, and my skin tingled. My heartbeat sped to an upbeat tempo, and my chest grew heavy.

I let go of Charles's hand and used mine to steady myself, splaying my hands out and grasping at whatever my fingers came into contact with. It felt like the car was spinning wildly out of control, but that was ridiculous. We were simply sitting here, side by side, with the engine shut off. I knew that and yet...

Charles said something, but I couldn't make sense of the words. What was happening to me?

A million thoughts rushed through my mind, but I couldn't grab onto any of them long enough for it to stick.

Paisley barked wildly. Charles continued talking to me in a steady, soothing voice. But I kept spiraling into an idle chaos, unmoored in a storm only I could sense.

It wasn't until Octo-Cat climbed out of the back seat and settled himself on my chest that my breathing, heart rate, and everything else began to slow back to a reasonable pace.

I listened to him purr as I closed my eyes and rested my cheek on his fur and felt the vibrations warm my skin. "What happened?" I asked when I finally felt like myself again.

"I'm pretty sure you just had a panic attack," Charles said carefully. He didn't reach for me like he normally would but rather gave me some space to recover. "Are you okay?"

"I think so," I told him and then lifted my face to look at the cat sitting on my chest.

This was so much like the first time I'd met Octavius that I almost felt *déjà vu*. I'd had a medical issue, come to with him on my chest. The only thing missing was...

"I'm hungry," he said, emitting a noxious cloud of day-old lobster roll breath. "How long has it been since you last fed me?"

"Yup, there it is," I said aloud, nodding once even though I was only confirming it to myself.

"What?" Charles asked, reaching forward slowly before rubbing my arm in a steady, soothing motion.

"Cats will be cats," I said with a small smile. For all his faults, Octo-Cat was someone I could always count on to be himself. And that made marching into the unknown easier, knowing that stability was never more than a furry companion away.

"How did he know to do that?" Charles asked, assessing the tabby.

"Who, me?" the cat asked, then stood and moved onto my lap to look out the window.

"Happened to Ethel from time to time," he said while staring off into the distance. "Whenever she started breathing funny, she'd grab me and hold on tight. Eventually she would feel better. Figured it would work on you, too. You know, since all humans are pretty much the same."

Funny how even after all our time together, Octo-Cat could still surprise me. I liked that. And I appreciated him now more than ever. For all his bluster, he still cared about me and was always there for me whenever it really counted.

He was here now, which meant I could do this.

I could meet my grandmother.

Learn the truth.

And keep on living my life.

It didn't have to change me.

And I had a feeling my merry crew of tagalong companions wouldn't let that happen, anyway.

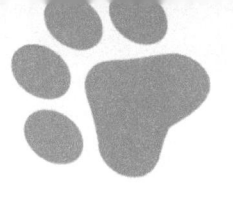

12

Charles held my hand while I clutched Paisley to my chest with my free arm. Octo-Cat nosed around the shrubs in pursuit of a fat robin.

"Okay," I said on the wings of an exhale.

Charles raised his finger and poked at the doorbell.

I focused on his fingers laced through mine, on Paisley shaking with excitement, on Octo-Cat making that ridiculous cat call that was meant to sound like a bird and lure them into his deadly clutches.

I listened for footsteps hurrying toward the door, but none came.

"Maybe it's broken," Charles said with a shrug

before tapping his knuckles against the door three times in rapid succession.

"Aww, you scared it away," Octo-Cat whined, pulling himself onto the cement stoop to stand beside us.

I didn't bother to translate, but I did set Paisley down and tried pounding on the door myself.

"I want to help!" Paisley said before letting out a string of high-pitched barks.

"Make it stop. Make it stop," Octo-Cat groaned and rolled onto his back, wiggling his spine against the pavement.

Still, my grandma didn't come to the door.

"Okay, so she's not home right now," Charles said, turning back toward the street. "Let's take a walk around the complex. See if we can learn anything from the neighbors."

I nodded as he tugged me after him.

Paisley scampered after us, and Octo-Cat returned to the shrubs.

"I'm going to wait for that robin to come back. Let me know when it's time to go," he said before pouncing out of sight.

"You don't think she's avoiding me, do you?" I asked Charles as we rounded the block.

He shook his head emphatically. "Why would

she do that? She doesn't even know you're coming, for starters, but also I'm sure she's dying to meet you. Why else would she have moved so close?"

She had moved close. For some reason, I hadn't considered that fact before. Hope filled my chest. "Do you think she might be looking for me and my mom, too?"

"Anything's possible." Charles picked up the pace. "Oh, look. There's someone out watering the grass."

A middle-aged man wearing cargo shorts and a sports T-shirt stood in brightly colored crocs with a hose in one hand and a cigarette in the other.

"Excuse me, sir!" Charles called, raising his free hand.

"If Susie sent you, you can forget about serving me with any more papers," the man snarled. I guess Charles gave off that attorney vibe even when he wasn't anywhere near the office.

"No, I don't work for Susie or anyone else. We're just here to see one of your neighbors. Could you tell me about—?"

The man raised his hand. "That's enough right there. If it's about a neighbor, it doesn't concern me, and I have enough trouble of my own without sticking my nose into anyone else's business. So just go on. Keep walking. Find some other poor sap, but you won't get a peep out of me."

I pulled Charles ahead. "Sorry to bother you!" I called to the man.

"Hey, you! Get that overgrown rat of yours off my lawn!" the man raged from somewhere behind us.

Charles and I turned back just in time to see Paisley lift her leg and let out a mighty stream of pee right beside the spot the angry guy had been watering.

He turned his hose on her and she ran away yipping.

"Good dog," I whispered when she caught up to us.

"I thought only male dogs lifted their legs to pee," Charles said rather than remarking on the man's defensiveness.

"Little dogs do it, too. You know, to put some space between themselves and the ground," I explained.

"Ah," was all he said to that.

We walked in silence for a while until we came upon a couple jogging.

Charles tried to flag them down, but they both pointed to their headphones and made to run past us. Surprising me and the joggers, Charles threw himself in their way, forcing them to stop.

"What's your problem, buddy?" The man loomed over us, ready for a fight.

"I'm just trying to get some information," Charles said, taking a step back. "We're looking—"

"Mitch. Yeah, he's just over there watering his grass," the man growled, pointing a meaty finger back in the direction from where we'd just come. "That's who you're looking for."

"That's who you guys are always looking for," the woman parroted with poorly concealed disgust. "Sue ought to just let up on the poor guy, but you vultures are all the same. As long as your invoices are paid, you keep on keeping on. How does it feel to ruin people's lives just to cut a paycheck?"

"We're not lawyers," I shouted in exasperation. "Well, Charles is, but that's not why we're here. We're looking for the woman that lives in the apartment with all the flamingos. Her name is Lyn Jones."

Both of them made faces like they'd just smelled something horrible.

"Her?" the guy asked.

"We don't know her and don't care to."

The woman scowled. "Yeah. Why would we?

All those lawn ornaments? Yuck. As if this neighborhood wasn't bad enough."

They continued to bicker between themselves about new people coming into the neighborhood and messing up the good dynamic they had going.

"Thank you," I said with a sigh.

If they heard me, they didn't show it. The couple took off jogging again, leaving Charles and me standing there dumbfounded.

"Care to keep trying?" Charles asked, shaking his head. "Three strikes before we're out of here?"

"I don't think I can take another strike right now," I answered. The last thing I wanted was another panic attack.

He didn't even question my decision.

Together, we returned to the unit with the pink flamingos to collect Octo-Cat and the car. I tried the door one last time since we were there already.

When my knocks went unanswered, I chewed my lip, then said, "I'm going to try calling her again."

The phone rang and rang, but only on the other end of the call, not inside the house.

Charles frowned. "Like I said, it's possible I got the location wrong. After all, Bravo's instructions were pretty hard to follow."

"No, this is it." I wasn't sure how I knew this was the place, but something deep inside me refused to be deterred. Besides, just how many stick-colored houses were there with pink sentinels standing guard around this place?

"Why don't we head back to the bed-and-breakfast and get some lunch?" Charles suggested as he opened the car door for me and the animals.

"Finally, UpChuck is good for something," Octo-Cat meowed as he settled himself into the back seat. "What are the chances we can find some lobst—?"

"No," I cut him off. "Hey, Charles. Which place had the good fries?" I said, suddenly craving something salty.

"My darling, I thought you'd never ask," he quipped, and we were off.

13

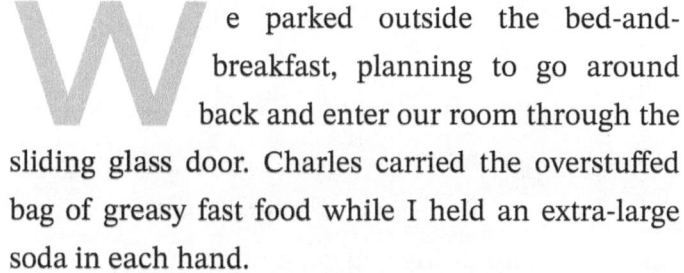

We parked outside the bed-and-breakfast, planning to go around back and enter our room through the sliding glass door. Charles carried the overstuffed bag of greasy fast food while I held an extra-large soda in each hand.

I'd planned on feeding the pets food we'd brought from home, but Octo-Cat had argued with me unrelentingly until I acquiesced, agreeing to purchase him a fish filet. We grabbed a plain burger for Paisley, too, since it would have been unfair not to treat her as well.

It wasn't a total defeat on my part, though. I made them both swear up and down they'd eat their pet food the rest of the time we were here.

"C'mon, let's get to the room before these babies get cold." Charles preferred that no one eat in his car, so we'd kept the bag sealed tight for the entire drive back, the delicious scents tormenting me the whole way.

A flash of orange caught my eye. At first I thought it was Louis the cat, but then I realized it was Millicent who had been watching us.

"And just where have you two been all morning?" she demanded, wrapping her long, red fingernails around a can of Diet Coke.

"Oh, here and there," I said with a shrug, then turned away.

But Millicent followed us, her flip-flops slapping against the gravel. "You weren't up to anything illegal, were you? Why, just last night I had a guest tell me her diamond ring had gone missing."

I gaped at her. "That was me. My ring went missing."

She balked, then sputtered as she searched for words. "Well, what did you do with it? Come out with it, then."

"I tried to tell you all of this last night. Weren't you listening? I took it off to get some sleep, then when I woke up it was gone."

She considered this before narrowing her eyes

and demanding, "How do I know you're not trying to frame my establishment just so you can collect the insurance money and get something better?"

"Are you actually serious right now?" I exploded. She was lucky my hands were full, or I'd —Okay, I wouldn't actually do anything untoward, but sometimes it was nice to pretend that I might.

"C'mon, Angie," Charles urged, tugging at my elbow and motioning with his chin. "Our lunch is getting cold."

"But she can't talk to us like that," I insisted, returning the cruel woman's glare. "See, this is why I'm guessing you don't get many return guests. Personal items go missing, the doors don't work, and you're one of the rudest people I've ever met!"

"I can't believe *you* would talk to *me* like that," Millicent snarled. "I don't have to let you stay here. In fact, pack your bags and—"

"No," I said firmly. "I'm not going anywhere until my ring is returned. So if you want to get rid of me, I suggest you find it first. Now good day, Millicent."

I stormed off with Charles and the animals in silent pursuit.

"Meee-yeow," Octo-Cat said, then let out a low whistle. "I've never been more proud of you,

Angela. It seems I have taught you something, after all."

"Yeah, well. Don't get used to it," I said, kicking off my shoes and slumping down onto the bed. My heart was beating like crazy again. I needed to stop getting so keyed up before it sent me to an early grave.

The toilet flushed in our connected bathroom, and I tensed up even more. "Who's there?" I shouted, still teetering on the edge.

The door burst open, and Sharon stepped out with her hands raised in the air. "Sorry, sorry. That glass door was open, so I let myself in. I wanted to apologize for how we left things yesterday and check to see how you're feeling today. Did you meet your grandmother? How did it go?"

Charles motioned for Sharon to join us and handed her a large container of fries.

"Oh, no. I didn't mean to intrude," Sharon began to argue, batting her eyelashes.

Charles pushed the fries at her again. "It's okay. I had at least five servings yesterday as part of my search. I'm all fried out."

She studied him with a furrowed brow. "That's a bit... odd. What do you mean you—?"

"Thanks for coming by," I blurted out, drawing

her attention back to me. "We went to her house, but nobody was home."

She frowned. "Oh."

"Yeah, and she's still not picking up her phone, so we're kind of stuck."

"Oh, boo." Her features crumpled into an even deeper frown. It was totally at odds with her usual free-spirited style. And so was her current outfit for that matter.

I looked the gray suit up and down, pausing briefly to take in the bright red clogs. "Sharon, what are you—?"

"Wearing?" she finished for me, her smile returning. "I have a meeting with the show's publicist, and I had no idea what they wanted from me, so a nice lady at the store helped me select this business suit. I hate it, but hopefully it will show I'm good at taking direction. She gave me shoes, too, but they were terribly uncomfortable. Luckily these clogs from my visit to New Amsterdam paired nicely." She paused to suck in a quick breath. "I know Chessy is the star, but I'm the one who signed all the papers, so..."

"You look great, Sharon," Charles said with a friendly grin. "Very professional."

She blushed mightily. "Why, thank you, kind sir."

Charles shifted his weight on the bed, jostling me in the process. Sharon sat opposite us on Octo-Cat's bed while he worked on his fish filet on the floor.

"Hey, Sharon," Charles said, balling up his burger wrapper and tossing it back in the bag. "While we have you here, maybe you can help us with something."

Sharon straightened her posture and placed her hands in her lap. "Anything." She was batting her eyelashes again. Oh, brother.

"You said you found some information about Marilyn's trials," Charles reminded her.

"Yes, but the records were sealed."

This didn't deter Charles one bit. "I may be able to get around that, if I find the right people to ask."

Sharon and I both looked to Charles askance.

He waved off our concern. "If I can find out where any of the cases took place, I can contact the prosecutor's office and let them know I'm working on a family case. See what they can tell me."

"Sure, let me just email you my notes," Sharon said, pulling out her phone. When that was taken care of, she leaned toward me. "Not only is he handsome, he's brilliant, too," Sharon confided in me with a whisper more than loud enough for Charles to hear too.

This time Charles was the one to blush mightily.

Octo-Cat's muffled voice rose to meet my ears. "And here I thought you were the only one crazy enough to join the UpChuck fan club," he said around a mouth full of food. "Looks like you aren't even the president, anymore."

This was getting ridiculous. I wasn't threatened in the least, but I still scooted closer to Charles on the bed and rested my head on his shoulder.

"You are a lucky, lucky girl, Angie Russo," Sharon said. "Now don't you forget to invite me to the wedding. It is my new life mission to land myself an uncle or a cousin. If they're half as perfect as your Charles, I'll die a happy woman... Now let me see that beautiful ring of yours again."

"Um, actually, it disappeared while I was taking a nap," I admitted with a frown.

"It's missing?" Sharon's eyes widened and she let out a huff. "Well, it's got to be around here somewhere. Want me to help you look?" she offered, sliding off the bed and onto her feet.

I stood, too. "Yeah, we searched everywhere, but—"

Sharon nodded sympathetically, then glanced toward the digital clock that hung on the wall opposite. "Oh, shoot! I can't stay to help, or I'll be late! Call me later! We'll find that ring—and that grandmother—yet. Don't you fret!"

And then Sharon ran off so fast that I didn't even have a chance to say goodbye.

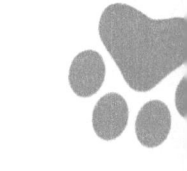

14

"That was weird," I said, watching as the glass door bounced back open following Sharon's sudden departure.

"You don't think she...?" Charles let his words trail away as he got up to push the door shut as best he could.

I tilted my head and scowled at him. "Are you actually suggesting she stole my ring?"

"She doesn't seem to have a problem entering without permission, and well..." His words fell away again, and he shrugged.

"She has a big, fat crush on you. Is that what you wanted to say? That she is so smitten for you that she stole the ring so she can fantasize about being your bride?"

"Smitten *with*," Charles corrected with a sigh. "And, well, it sounds stupid when you say it like that, but it's not like we have any other leads to go on."

"Sharon is my friend," I reminded him. "If anyone stole my ring, it's that nasty Millicent." True, Sharon had only been my friend for a week, but she'd made up for her bad first impression, unlike the owner of this bed-and-breakfast who just kept making things worse every time we ran into her.

Charles sat back on the bed and placed an arm around my shoulders. "We'll find it. I promise, but let's try to figure this thing out with your grandma first, okay?"

I nodded. "You're right. One thing at a time."

"Exactly." He got up to retrieve his work bag.

"So, I guess, you see what you can learn from what Sharon gave you, and I'll check her social media."

"Mommy!" Paisley let out a sharp bark to get my attention. "May I please go outside to play?"

"Right, okay." I opened the door for her and watched her frolic toward the sandy beach. "I think I'll go out, too. Keep an eye on her," I told Charles.

"Come get me when you're ready to head back out?"

He gave me a hearty thumbs-up. He'd already pulled his laptop out and situated it onto his lap. You can take the guy out of the office, but getting the office out of the guy was a whole different story. Charles's lawyer skills had come in handy many times before, and they just might be the thing to save the day now.

I'd be gutted if we had to leave Katahdin without ever meeting my grandmother. We just had to find her. We had to, and we would.

I approached the lake and found Paisley digging a hole in the sand. She didn't even notice me as I approached.

"What's that?" I asked when she pulled her head out with a small, black object in her mouth.

"It's a pretty rock," she mumbled, accidentally dropping her prize when she did. She yipped in surprise, grabbed it back up, and ran off with tail wagging. I was fairly certain my nan's dog had just unearthed a clam but had no idea what she was actually doing with it. It's not like she'd be able to crack open the hard shell and get at the meat inside.

I shrugged and continued cutting a path toward

the dock. Well, whatever Paisley was up to, at least she was happy about it. Sometimes I envied her, how easy it was for her to see the best in every situation.

Me, on the other hand, I had a hard time not worrying about what would come next. Especially now.

I'd told Charles I would check Grandma Marilyn's social media. Mostly it was because I'd have felt guilty if he dug deep into research while I sat around twiddling my thumbs.

Of course, I'd already checked her social media as soon as I knew her current name and location. I'd tried to find her before last night, but Jones wasn't exactly an uncommon surname. I finally managed to find the correct profile yesterday evening while I was supposed to be relaxing in the tub.

Unfortunately, my grandmother hadn't posted a single photo of herself during all her years on the site, assigning a simple stock-image daisy to serve as her profile picture.

She also rarely updated her status. When I checked last night, the most recent one had been made about eight months ago—commentary on some TV show she'd just started watching on some cable channel I'd never heard of.

I navigated to her profile now, expecting to see the exact same feed.

But no.

My grandma had posted an update less than an hour ago. We'd probably just left her neighborhood at the time. *Whoa.*

"Nothing beats sunny skies and sandy beaches! Hello, San Francisco!" she'd captioned a photo of the Golden Gate bridge.

Wow. Was she really clear on the other side of the country?

What dumb luck.

Of course, California made sense. Her phone had a Cali area code. Hey, maybe she was planning to move back and change her name again.

Then I'd never find her.

I scrolled through my newsfeed idly, completely frustrated with this turn of events and wondering how I would break it to Charles, especially considering that we'd lost my engagement ring because of our trip out here. And it hadn't even been a full week since he'd proposed.

Ugh. I was the worst fiancée ever.

Tears stung at the edges of my eyes, and I didn't try to hold them back. Stupid San Francisco, I thought, looking for someone to blame other than myself.

Then, for whatever reason, I navigated back to my grandmother's profile to look at that picture again. Perhaps it was just to wallow in my dumb luck, or maybe I'd subconsciously realized that something didn't quite add up.

That's when I saw it. She'd checked in when she posted the photo, not at the Golden Gate bridge in San Francisco, but at the Golden Wok in Katahdin, Maine.

Oh my gosh.

She was here—here and lying about it.

When she'd tried to pull up the Golden Gate bridge, the social media site must have brought up nearby establishments with similar names. My grandmother hadn't noticed that the geo-tag gave her away.

But why would she lie about being out of town?

"Hi, Mommy!" Paisley called as she rushed past me, then dipped her head and picked up a pink shell, only to immediately take off running again.

"Hi," I called back distractedly. My grandmother was here, and she knew I was looking for her.

She wanted to put me off her scent, but I

refused to go home without meeting her first. Maybe she'd never want to see me again after—and that possibility hurt me deeply—but, still, I at least had to try.

I'd rather meet her and have it go badly than never get the chance at all.

Now I just had to tell Charles what I'd found, and we could figure out our next steps from there.

15

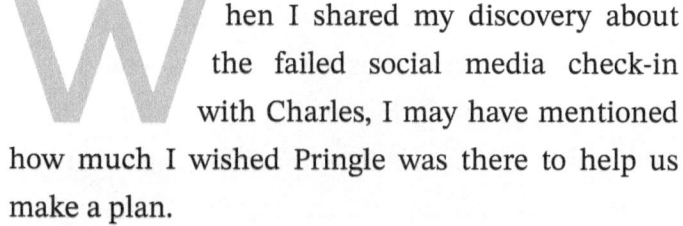

When I shared my discovery about the failed social media check-in with Charles, I may have mentioned how much I wished Pringle was there to help us make a plan.

And Octo-Cat took the bait, hook, line, and sinker.

"The dog and I are better than that raccoon fraud could ever hope to be," he growled and then insisted he could handle things from here.

We drove back out to the condominium complex, and I watched as the pets tore away from the car to begin their top-secret recon mission. Octo-Cat had declared the details of the operation to be on a need-to-know basis and then had proceeded to explain that I did not need to know.

Charles reached over and squeezed my knee.

With growing trepidation, I closed the door so that he could drive us around the corner and out of sight.

The part of the plan that I'd been privy to involved Charles and me circling the block slowly while the animals followed through with their mission to track down my missing grandmother.

"Am I wrong for kind of wishing the raccoon was with us?" Charles asked later with a snort. "At least he keeps things interesting."

By this point, we'd driven around the neighborhood at least a dozen times, and the residents had noticed. If we kept this up much longer, we'd soon have a cop car on our tail.

"You know I only brought up Pringle to get Octo-Cat to think helping us was his idea, right?" I reminded him with a laugh. "So, yes, you are very wrong for thinking Pringle's presence would improve anything. You don't have to listen to him prattle on the way the rest of us do. Do you know during our last trip, he decided to pick up trucker lingo?"

Charles burst out laughing. "You're kidding. Why didn't you tell me earlier?"

"I've tried my best to block it out, honestly. He was going on and on about Smokeys and ten fours and whatever else. I couldn't manage to understand the half of it."

"Huh. Makes me wonder if you could understand animals speaking a foreign language. Like—"

"Stop the car!" I shouted as I spotted the waggy black blur of Paisley rushing down the sidewalk barking at us.

"Mommy! Mommy! Mommy! Mommy!" I heard her crying as soon as the door opened.

"I'll park the car and catch up," Charles called as I jumped out of the car.

"What's going on, Paisley?" The little dog leapt into my arms and frantically licked my face.

"We found her! We found your grandmama," the Chihuahua yipped excitedly. "Follow me!"

She leapt from my arms and began sprinting at full tilt. I glanced back to make sure Charles was coming before I started running after the quivering bullet of a dog.

I sprinted after Paisley, thankful for the time Nan had forced me to work out with her friend's dog Cujo for a time. Of course, the husky had moved at a steady, even clip, unlike the wildly darting mini-dog I was attempting to follow now.

My current canine guide also didn't seem to worry much about the obstacles I was having trouble getting around, over, and under. The first thing I tripped over was a sprinkler, and it sent me crashing down onto the same lawn that belonged to that grumpy guy we'd met earlier. Why? Just why?

Staggering back to my feet, very little time passed before I crashed headlong into a raspberry bush.

Meanwhile, Paisley remained blissfully unaware of my challenges and of how far I'd fallen behind. The little dog's legs were almost invisible with her sprinting, hopping gait.

Trying to focus on Paisley meant not paying enough attention to the road ahead of me, and I thumped into a set of garbage cans, then jammed my knee into a fence post.

Maybe we should have followed her in the car. Too late for that now, I guessed.

Off-balance and disoriented, I was overwhelmed when I saw that Paisley was no longer surging forward. She now ran tight circles behind one of the condos.

"Mommy! Mommy!" she yelled. "It's right here! This is the place!"

And there was my grandmother, sitting at a small patio table with Octo-Cat, who was happily munching on a shrimp cocktail. I stood there, woozily, my mouth opening and closing without any sound coming out. It would so leave the wrong impression if I threw up now.

Octo-Cat looked up at me and yawned before licking the sauce off his paw.

"Angela," he purred. "This is your grandma Lyn. Lyn, Angela."

"Hello, Angela," Lyn said, almost as if she were responding to Octo-Cat. "Sorry for giving you the runaround, dear. I'm... Well, I was afraid you'd be disappointed, and I couldn't stand the thought of you rejecting me."

My heart felt like it was breaking for her. She had been just as worried about meeting me as I'd been about meeting her.

But before I could find something to say, she continued. "I was tipped off that you were heading my way when your friend... Um, what was her name again?"

"Sharon," Octo-Cat replied.

"Ah, Sharon," Lyn said as if prompted by Octo-Cat. "The reality star that was looking into me wasn't the subtlest of people. So I knew you were coming here. When I saw you and your fellow sitting out in your car for so long, I knew it just had to be you."

She poured more iced tea into her glass and added a few more shrimp to Octo-Cat's cocktail.

"Of course, the moment you got out, I knew for certain. The family genes are extremely strong. You look so much like my sister did when we were growing up. But I'm sure that's not why you made the trip out here."

"Of course not," Octo-Cat said, polishing off another shrimp. "We were here to find out why your husband decided to take your child and make a run for it."

I winced at Octo-Cat's bluntness.

"Relax, Angela. I understand how cats can be," Lyn said, clucking her tongue and shaking her head. "And for the record, you're right, Octavius. I lost my dear little Laura because her father didn't believe me when I told him I could talk to animals. Such a shame."

Whoa. I still hadn't even said so much as hello,

and already my grandmother had told me her big secret.

It was a secret we shared.

Did this mean...? Could I talk to animals because she could? I couldn't wait to hear more.

16

A few minutes later, Lyn handed me an old photograph and a fresh glass of iced tea. She handed a second glass to Charles, settled back into her chair, and pulled Octo-Cat onto her lap.

I expected him to object, but he simply curled up and began purring.

"That's your mother," she said wistfully. "It was the only picture I had of her for so many years until I found her on the news. There's so much I missed from all of your lives. But I guess I understand. Your grandfather wasn't a bad man. He was just scared."

I nodded along. Gosh, I just loved listening to her voice. She could talk forever, and I'd be her willing captive.

"It all started when I was working at the diner to pay my way through college," Grandma Marilyn continued. "Jimmy, the owner, was a good enough guy, but he was also a cheapskate." She glanced at me over the edge of her glasses, and I laughed. "He wanted to fix every last little thing himself. Said repair shops were all a scam to bilk the working man out of his hard-earned money.

"So when the power cord to our industrial sized coffee maker got frayed, Jimmy fixed it. It didn't work that well, but cheap was better than good, if you asked him. As for me, I ended up taking quite a shock. When I woke up, I found the world a lot noisier than it had been."

"Me, too!" I squealed, standing up and jabbing my thumb into my chest. "Oh my gosh, it was the exact same!"

Grandma Marilyn laughed. "Yes, Every animal was talking and the problem was that only I could understand what they were saying. I tried to keep it secret for as long as I could, but when animals know you can talk to them, they won't leave you alone. I'm sure you understand that.

"William tried to be understanding. After all, we'd been together a short time and he thought maybe it was just overwork or some sort of 'female thing' that was causing me to think I could understand animals. And the doctors, they agreed with him. Claimed it was some sort of pregnancy-induced hysteria. Times were different back then. I didn't have many rights as a young, unwed mother-to-be. William had done right by me and proposed. Our wedding wasn't far off, either, until I started talking to cats and dogs. Then he found one reason after another to delay. And then with the doctors involved, I wound up on bed rest and drugged out of my mind on who knows what kind of drugs.

"I barely remember giving birth to Laura. In fact, for a time, William convinced me that I'd never been pregnant in the first place. I can't really be mad at him. He thought he was helping me. If he didn't really love me, I'm sure he would've just had me committed and taken off. But, though we never did make it official via marriage, he stuck with me through it all. Trying to fix me. Trying to get rid of the voices in my head."

I squeezed Charles's hand under the table.

My Grandma continued on, her eyes dry. As tragic as this tale was, she'd lived it. She'd already come to terms with how her life had turned out.

"For ten years I was in and out of institutions.

Bouncing from one diagnosis to another. Schizophrenia, multiple personality disorder, psychosis, detachment from reality. They threw everything at the wall to see what stuck.

"We ended up out in California of all places when I managed to talk to a desert cottontail. He was very different from any of the animals I'd spoken to before, and it sort of clicked in my mind that I wasn't crazy, no matter how long doctors and my beau had been trying to convince me otherwise.

"I broke out of the hospital and went on the run. It was much easier in those days. No cell phones, no electronic credit card monitoring. It took actual phone calls and detective work to track down someone that didn't want to be found.

"Sure, I hit a few speed bumps along the way, a couple of arrests and some close calls with my abilities, but I learned how to hide it from everyone, and I tried to appear normal for a time. Not much of a life, I know, but I was at least out of the hospitals.

"Of course, old William felt guilty and eventually tracked me down to a small town near the Florida-Georgia border. Gave me this picture of Laura, thanked me for letting him go so that he could find someone else. He said he still loved me, but that we weren't any good for each other.

"I never saw him again after that. But knowing that your mother was out there, I had at last found a purpose. I drifted from town to town, doing whatever work I could find and making friends with any animals that might be able to help me track down my daughter.

"That's actually why I've got such a large collection of flamingos out front. Each one represents a close friend I've made along the way. Of course, wild flamingos only live to be about twenty, so sadly, that display is more like a memorial."

She leaned forward and steepled her fingers. "Angela. I don't know how to tell you this, but having this gift is a lonely life. Sure, you can talk to all the animals, but you really miss out on the human connections that give life meaning. And that's why I was so worried you would reject me. No one wants a crazy old woman in their family tree."

"I do," I said, unshed tears blurring my vision. "I want it more than anything."

"I do, too, sweetie. When Octavius here told me you and I shared more than just a passing genetic resemblance, I thought maybe, just maybe I'd found my family again."

I offered her a smile that started small but then

grew to take up a huge portion of my face. I'd sat transfixed for her entire story, and now I just couldn't help it—I threw my arms around her and gave my grandmother a hug.

The first of what I hoped would be many.

"I'm so glad I found you," I whispered, not wanting to let go.

"Thank you for not giving up on me. I can't have made it easy."

"Actually, when you have a moment, I'd like to teach you about social media safety. That way, the next time you want to hide from someone, you don't make the same silly mistake." I explained how I'd determined she wasn't really out of town, and together we shared a great big belly laugh.

We sat at that rickety patio set for hours, sharing stories of our lives, telling her about what Charles and I hoped for with our wedding, and of course, remembering all the weird and wonderful animals who had enriched our lives along the way.

"Do you promise you'll come back tomorrow?" my grandma asked after we all shared a delicious dinner of grilled chicken and vegetables.

"You couldn't keep her away if you tried," Charles promised, pulling me into his side as we both stood.

"I know that," Grandma Marilyn said. "I already tried and failed."

We all laughed again and said goodnight. This didn't feel like a first meeting. It felt like coming home.

Like family.

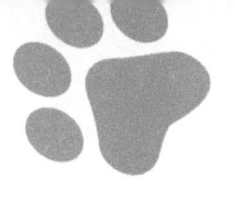

17

Charles and I returned to the bed and breakfast well after dinnertime, both with huge smiles on our faces.

"What a day," he said.

"Yeah," I said back. It was all either of us needed to express. Our time with my grandmother had said it all.

"I liked Grandma Lyn," Paisley said as I lifted her into my arms and climbed out of the car.

"She reminded me of Ethel," Octo-Cat remarked, drawing Paisley's and my eyes to him.

I didn't say anything because we were no longer in the privacy of the car, and Millicent had already proven she wasn't above spying.

"Hang on a sec," I told Charles and waited.

Luckily, Octo-Cat didn't hesitate to continue. "What?" he asked, stretching in the backseat while we all waited on him. "She's a nice, old lady. A nice, old, relatively normal lady. Also, she had tea."

"I don't know why I was expecting something more profound," I murmured to myself.

Paisley squirmed within my arms. "What about the *pound?*"

I patted her head. "Everything is perfectly fine. Let's head back to our room," I said while looking at Charles, just in case Millicent was watching.

The gravel crunched at the edge of the lot as another car pulled in. And not just any car—a police car.

"I smell trouble," Octo-Cat said with a grin, hopping out of the car and craning his neck to see better while hiding behind my legs. Always hungry for someone else's drama, that one.

Millicent spilled forth from the entryway, waving her arms overhead. "Officer, officer! This is them!" It looked as if she'd taken great care with her appearance, considering the obscene amount of both makeup and jewelry she now wore. She'd been expecting us.

The policeman unfurled himself from the driver's seat, reaching an impressive height, close to seven feet, if I had to guess. He tucked his thumbs into his belt loop and approached me and Charles.

Paisley shook and squirmed, not because she was frightened but simply because she was eager to say hello to the new arrival.

Clearly a dog person, the cop reached over and scratched under her chin with his thick fingers, then pulled back and glared down at Charles. "You been giving Mrs. Strobel trouble?"

"No, sir," he said, standing in place, far more calm and collected than I could ever be in this type of situation.

"Are you kidding me?" I boomed.

Millicent ran in front of us, shouting, "Yes! Yes, they have! Then they refused to leave when I asked them to. That's why I'd like you to escort them from the property!"

The officer glanced at each of us in turn, finally deciding on Charles as the most rational one among us. "Would you like to tell me what happened here today?" he asked, pulling out a notebook that looked comically small in his oversized hands.

Charles didn't miss a beat. "My fiancée's engagement ring went missing," he explained, taking care not to talk with his hands the way he usually did. "We reported it to Mrs. Strobel immediately upon discovering its absence last night."

The officer bobbed his head. "And then?"

"This afternoon, we returned from meeting a friend when Mrs. Strobel met us outside the bed-and-breakfast, demanding to know where we had gone and whether we'd engaged in any illegal activity. She then accused us of stealing the ring, not realizing that we were the same ones who'd reported it missing. When we pointed this out, she accused us of implicating her establishment in a planned insurance fraud, which I can assure you is not accurate."

The officer raised one eyebrow. "Then?"

"Then she demanded we leave. Naturally, since we had booked our reservation for two nights, we didn't see any reason to check out before said duration. Also, my fiancée was not eager to leave before we could find her missing engagement ring."

"Uh-huh. Then?" He glanced sidelong at Millicent, who stood openly scowling at Charles.

"We had lunch with a friend in our room, went back out to visit the same friend that we'd gone to see that morning, and then returned, leading to present circumstances," Charles concluded.

Millicent shook a finger at us. The sleeves of her

oversized mint silk blouse belled in the wind. "You see that? They have too many friends! I don't trust them one bit!"

The policeman shifted his posture slightly so that he was facing Millicent. "Ma'am, what evidence do you have that these two guests of yours faked the disappearance of their engagement ring?"

She patted her stomach furiously. "I don't need any evidence. I feel it all right here. In my gut! Always go with your gut!"

The officer pressed his lips into a firm line. "Unfortunately, that's not how the law works. Without any evidence to go on, I won't be able to follow through on your request. Also, it seems to me that you are, in fact, the one in the wrong here."

Her jaw fell open. "What?" she barely managed to gasp. I was guessing that neither Millicent's brain nor her lungs were getting much oxygen in that moment.

"Quite simply put, you're harassing these people."

She shook her head, apparently too angry to argue. Well, good, because I was more than done here.

"There's something else, too," Charles shot in, finally speaking freely again, hands and all. "A case of gross negligence. You see, there's this problem with our door..."

I listened with a smug grin as Charles went on to describe our issue with both the front door and the side door for our room. He also filed a formal police report about my missing ring.

At some point, Millicent stormed off. If she hadn't hated us before, she definitely did now.

Charles and I laughed the whole thing off as we made our way back to the room. Not even Millicent's ridiculous antics could spoil the wonderful day we'd had with my grandmother.

"That plan backfired on her, huh?" Charles asked with a wink.

"Oh, spectacularly!" I giggled. "And I loved every moment of it."

Suddenly, Paisley surged forward, barking as she ran. "Get away, you big bully!"

I just barely spotted the flash of orange as Louis scurried off into the night.

"Paisley!" I lifted her to my face and let her lick my cheeks. "I'm so proud of you! You stood up to him all on your own!"

"And don't come back!" she yelped into the night, clearly very pleased with herself.

"What a strange trip this has been," Charles said

as we finished the walk to our bedroom. The door, as always, was cracked partially open.

"Strange, but good," I added.

We bobbed our heads in agreement.

"But let's stay somewhere else next time we come to pay Grandma Marilyn a visit?" Charles wanted to clarify.

I grabbed his hand and planted a kiss on the back of it. "Definitely."

Next time we came for a visit, I already knew exactly where I'd be staying. Grandma Marilyn had invited us to come soon and often and said we always had a place to stay.

And who needs decently reviewed bed-and-breakfasts when you have family?

18

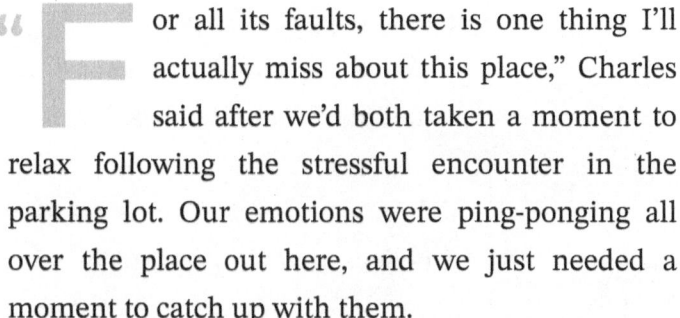

"For all its faults, there is one thing I'll actually miss about this place," Charles said after we'd both taken a moment to relax following the stressful encounter in the parking lot. Our emotions were ping-ponging all over the place out here, and we just needed a moment to catch up with them.

"Oh, yeah." I turned toward him with an expectant smile. "And what's that?"

His cheeks lifted in that signature smile I loved so much. "Beach access."

"There are a million beaches back in Glendale," I reminded him, wrinkling my nose playfully.

"Yeah, but none are right outside our back

door." He stood and offered me his hand. "One more moonlight stroll?"

"Oh, you hopeless romantic, you," I teased. Really, Sharon was right. I was, in fact, the luckiest woman alive.

I followed Charles in a lovesick daze until a short way from our room, I tripped and stumbled forward.

Thankfully my knight in shining armor caught me before I could connect with the ground.

"What was that?" I asked, glancing back but unable to see what had tripped me up.

Charles took out his cell phone and shone the flashlight onto a small pile of assorted beach bric-a-brac.

"Just some random nature stuff," he said with a shrug. "At least I believe that's the technical term for it."

"Wait," I shouted as he moved to slide his phone back into his pocket. "Go back over that stuff again, but a bit more slowly this time."

Charles shrugged and did as I asked, moving the light back and forth until it caught on a shiny black rock.

No, not a rock.

"That's a clam, right?" I asked, remembering the scene with Paisley earlier.

He shrugged again. "Yeah, I think so."

I ambled over and pointed at a pink shell. "And that's a shell?"

"Yes, that one I'm sure of. I'm absolutely certain that is a seashell." He poked me playfully in the side, but I was too focused to return his silliness in kind.

"Paisley," I called into the night, turning back toward our room, which was still in sight. The little black dog nudged the glass door open and then came bounding toward us.

"Yes, Mommy?" she asked, one ear tall and pointy and the other flopped forward.

"Do these things belong to you?" I said, motioning toward the upset pile.

"My treasures!" she cried, running to them and rolling around. "What happened?"

"Yup, that's what I thought. Case solved. Well, almost. Maybe. C'mon, we need to talk to Octo-Cat," I told Charles.

But Paisley whimpered and refused to follow along, "No, please don't tell him about my treasures. I don't want him to steal them from me like he does at home."

"I promise I won't tell him about your secret hoard," I assured the distraught pup.

She followed, albeit somewhat reluctantly.

"What's going on?" Charles wanted to know as we approached the cabin.

"I have an idea about what might have happened to my ring," I told him right as I pulled the door to our room wide open and the three of us stepped inside.

"What do you want now?" my cat demanded. "I thought I was finally getting a bit of me time, but noooo. Here you all are. Again. Story of all nine of my lives. Ugh." He let out a long sigh, but I refused to fall prey to his dramatics.

"You're a cat. Literally every second of every day is your you time," I told him.

Octo-Cat scoffed but said nothing more.

When it was clear he'd yielded the floor, I said, "Listen, I need your help."

"Yup, there it is!" he spat and flicked his tail. "You'd be lost without me, admit it."

"If I do, will you help?" If my pride was the price of his assistance, I'd happily give it up. I'd lived with a cat for long enough to know how this whole thing worked. Which meant I also expected what came next.

Octo-Cat flopped onto his side and yawned. "I'll think about it. Really, I'm quite tired. Between sleuthing and helping you sort out your cloying human emotion, you've been working me hard all weekend. I need some time to rest and recharge."

"Shut up, you!" Paisley barked and kicked her feet back. "If Mommy needs our help, then we're going to give it to her!"

"Paisley!" I said in shock. She almost never took a tough approach to anything, especially not when it involved the big feline brother she idolized.

Octo-Cat stared at Paisley with large amber eyes.

Paisley stared back with shiny black eyes.

And I couldn't believe what happened next.

"Whatever," Octo-Cat backed down, blinking his eyes slowly as he turned to me. "Just tell me what you need, so we can get this over with."

Knowing better than to waste time questioning the madness I'd just witness, I moved ahead with my original intent. First, I explained the theory I'd developed after stumbling over Paisley's beachy hoard, then I told them what I needed them to do.

Octo-Cat rolled onto his feet. "C'mon, Mutt. Let's go do the thing."

But Paisley didn't follow. "It hurts my feelings when you call me that," she said firmly.

Seriously? What the heck was going on here? Octo-Cat was showing his softer side while Paisley was standing up for herself. Nothing made sense anymore. Perhaps this place emanated some kind of strange magic.

Ha, as if!

Once the animals departed, Charles held his hand out to me. "Now about that walk."

19

"Is every trip with you going to be like this?" Charles asked, kissing the back of my hand.

"Yup, and you're stuck with me now," I laughed.

"I don't mind," he said, pulling me close to gaze into my eyes. "I know your grandmother had a hard time because of her gifts, but I want you to know that I plan to always be here for you, no matter what."

"Thank you," I said. "I can't imagine what it must've been like for her back then. To be so alone and for so long."

"Well, you might have to keep the secret from everyone else, but you've got a lot of us who are there for you."

"Yeah, I know, and I—"

"Mommy!" a little voice interrupted.

I pulled away from Charles and looked out into the night to see Paisley bounding up with Octo-Cat hot on her heels.

Octo-Cat held up a paw, struggling to catch his breath. "We...we...we found it. Which means... You owe me... A lobster roll."

"Okay, so where is it?" I asked, excitement crashing over me. Ahh, what a rush! This was one crime I couldn't wait to solve once and for all, not only because of what had been stolen but also because of who was at fault.

Tugging Charles along, I followed the pets inside and went over to the front desk where Millicent sat grumbling to herself while she read her book.

"Excuse me," I said, ringing the bell on the desk.

Millicent rolled her eyes and moved the bell. "Go away," she grumbled, adding in a few choice words under her breath.

"I just wanted to let you know that we've caught the thief that's been plaguing your bed-and-break-fast," I revealed with a self-satisfied smirk. Okay, so I wasn't being the most professional in that moment, but Millicent hadn't actually hired me, so

I was justified in my approach. At least that's what I told myself now.

"You've got a lot of nerve," she said, slamming her book onto the desk.

Instead of baiting the old woman further, I walked over to the antique armoire Octo-Cat and Paisley were patiently sitting by. I pulled on the door, and it swung open to reveal...nothing but an empty armoire.

"Behind it," Octo-Cat whispered.

"Oops," I said, closing the door. "Charles, could you help me here and move the armoire over a bit?"

Nodding his agreement, he got low on the furniture piece and slid it across the floor, revealing a large hole in the wall with a fat, orange cat asleep on a pile of valuables like a flugly—that's fluffy and ugly—dragon. Near the top of the horde sat my ring, shimmering in all its matrimonial magnificence.

"It looks like your cat has been taking things from your guests and stashing them here," I said, triumphantly plucking my ring from the pile and allowing Charles to slide it back onto my finger where it belonged.

The old lady's skin went pale, and she stammered a bit before finding her voice. "I'm so sorry.

To the both of you. I had no idea Louis was using his nap spot for something so... so... That's a bad kitty!" She scooped the pile out of the nook, jostling the cat from his place.

"I'm so sorry," she said again. "I honestly thought that my guests were lying and trying to sink my business. A developer had offered to buy the place a year ago, and I thought because I'd turned him down, he was trying to run me out of business. I guess that'll teach me to get too involved in my stories. Oh, I owe so many people apologies, and I've got to make sure all of these things get back to their rightful owners. Thank you so much for helping me out, and after I was so rude to you."

"So can we be friends now?" I asked.

Her face soured. "I still don't approve of your shenanigans. And also your beau scratched my floor when he moved that armoire. Expect the repairs to be added on to your bill."

My jaw dropped. From sour to sweet and back again almost instantaneously. I swear, there was no winning with some people.

"I still don't care for you much, but since you managed to help me, I'll let you stay until check-out tomorrow morning," she said reluctantly. "But I don't want you two back here until you're well and properly married. I run a wholesome business here. Now go, get out of here, before I change my mind."

Charles and I rushed away, laughing the whole time.

Millicent didn't know the first thing about us or our relationship, but she believed what she wanted to—and we had nothing to prove.

Now that I had my ring back, I counted this weekend a perfect success.

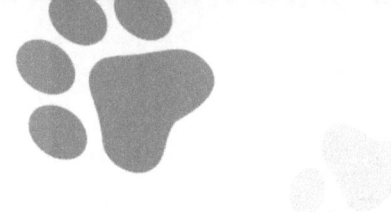

20

always loved getting away, but even more than that, I loved coming back home. My life rocked, now more than ever.

I was surprised to find Nan waiting up for me even though it was quite late. "How was your trip, dear?" she asked, stretching her arms overhead and standing to greet me.

"Did you get my message?" I asked, scooping her up in a hug.

"Yes, all seventeen of them. I'm sorry I didn't return any of them. This felt like a conversation we should have face to face."

Hmm, now where had I heard that before. Sharon. I'd need to call and give her an update since we were unable to meet up before Charles and I headed home again. I had a feeling we'd both be seeing a lot of her in our future, starting with our upcoming nuptials.

"Shall I put on some tea?" Nan offered, hooking her thumb toward the kitchen.

"No," I said, gently lowering myself onto the couch and patting the cushion beside me. If I gave Nan an excuse to put this off, she'd keep finding more and more reasons to put it off further. If we were going to have this talk, we needed to have it now.

I reached forward and grabbed both of her hands in mine, waiting for Nan to share what was on her mind.

"I'm sorry I kept you away from your grandmother all these years. It's the one thing in my life I truly regret," she said with a sigh.

I shook my head emphatically. "I don't."

She lifted her eyes to mine, searching. "What?"

"I don't regret you doing that, and neither should you."

Nan swallowed. "Was she really that terrible?"

"No, she was actually pretty cool." I smiled, remembering the moments we'd shared that weekend.

And Nan's expression pinched.

"But I'm glad I grew up with you," I quickly added. "Marilyn is nice, and I look forward to getting to know her much better, but you've helped shape my life into what it is today. And I love my life. I love you. I wouldn't have wanted anything different."

"Really?" Nan looked so frail in that moment. For the first time in a long time, I really saw her age. She'd lived through a lot and carried one very big secret for most of her life. How did she feel now that it had been exposed and that everyone still loved her just as much as before?

"Really, really," I said in a silly voice.

She laughed at my reference to an old movie we'd watched together countless times in my childhood.

"Will you believe me this time?"

Nan wiped away a tear, then grabbed my hands again and gave them a good squeeze. "I'll try."

"Well, that's the best any of us can do, right?" I winked. "Someone super smart and awesome taught me that."

"Speaking of all those lovely adjectives, how was she? Did you find out why William...?" She let her words trail off, unwilling—or perhaps unable—to voice what her late friend had done. With that single action, he'd changed all of our lives forever. We'd never know exactly why he'd done it, but I trusted Grandma Marilyn's interpretation of events. Of course, it led me to wonder if my missing grandpa would have accepted me for who I am, if he'd gotten the chance to meet me before he passed.

Sometimes I had a hard time remaining serious in serious moments. I knew a joke wouldn't help here, so I called upon my best impression of Charles. "Well, you see, the prevailing theory is that he took Mom away because he believed he was keeping her safe from Marilyn."

Nan's eyes bulged. "Was Marilyn dangerous? Is she now?"

I waggled my fingers. "She's kooky-crazy. Turns out she can talk to animals."

Nan gasped. "You can't be serious!"

I just smiled and nodded. "No one would believe her, including Grandpa. He chose never to see his own daughter again rather than to believe something so magical could be possible."

Nan gasped again. "Oh, that poor old man. He missed out on so much."

"It was his choice," I pointed out. "Marilyn never got a choice. You didn't have much of one, either."

"He made a choice, but it was the wrong one. That doesn't sound like the friend I knew. Still, I'm so incredibly grateful for the life we've shared."

"Me, too," I said, peppering her cheek with a kiss.

Nan shook her head and looked down at her lap. "You and Marilyn must have had a lot of stories to share."

"We did, and I really like her."

What Nan said next surprised me more than anything else had so far that weekend. "I think I would, too."

"Good, because she's coming over for dinner next month. I figured that would give everyone enough time to let everything sink in, and it's still well before the wedding. By the way, I have a new friend that I just know you're going to love. Her name is Sharon, and..."

We stayed up the whole night talking, just like the old days. I had a lot to tell my mom, but that could wait until tomorrow. She had her own feelings about our sordid history, and I'd have to find a way to help her work through them.

But that's what the people in your life were for.

They were there for you.

And it was okay to lean on them when you needed to.

I learned that this weekend, and I hoped with time my grandma Marilyn would be able to learn it, too.

I couldn't wait for her to meet the rest of the family, and I couldn't wait to delve further into our shared ability and what it could mean for us in the future.

Would Pet Whisperer P.I. get a new partner member?

Heck if I knew. But for once, not knowing was actually part of the fun.

Can Angie solve a new murder before her wedding?

Get your copy of *Deer Duplicity* so that you can keep reading this series today!

* * *

Pssst... If you absolutely loved this book and want even more, make sure you **sign up for Molly's**

newsletter. When you do, you'll receive an exclusive digital prize pack, including a free book!

WHAT'S NEXT?

Lately I've been putting my P.I. business on the back burner in favor of planning my upcoming nuptials. But when my brand-new next-door neighbor turns up dead, I drop everything to investigate—especially since I had a clear motive for her murder and I don't plan on saying "I do" in jail.

The police say her death was an accident, but it doesn't seem so open and shut to me. A frightened buck may be the only one who knows what really happened, but I'm having a hard time getting him to stop running and to start talking.

Another problem? Octo-Cat and I can't see eye-to-eye on how to tackle our newest investigation,

which forces me to work with my other, less reli-
able animal sidekicks to get the job done. Can I not
only prove foul play, but also solve the case?

DEER DUPLICITY is now available.

**Get your copy so that you can keep reading
this series today!**

SNEAK PEEK
DEER DUPLICITY

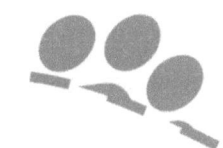

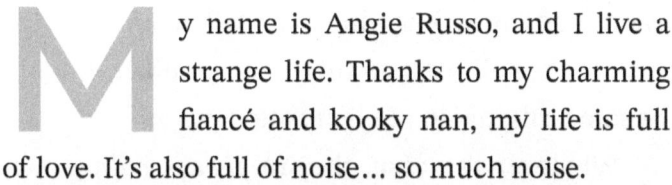

My name is Angie Russo, and I live a strange life. Thanks to my charming fiancé and kooky nan, my life is full of love. It's also full of noise... so much noise.

I can talk to animals, and once they find that out, most don't want to shut up. It all started with Octo-Cat. He and I met at a will reading, back when I was still working a temp job as a paralegal. His owner had just passed, and I'd just had an unfortunate run-in with a busted coffeemaker. Put the two together and—bam—our odd friendship was born. The first thing we did together was solve the murder of his former owner, which took some doing since everyone else happily assumed the old lady had died of natural causes.

Once I'd officially adopted my tabby companion, I became the trustee for his rather generous trust fund, and the two of us moved into his former owner's old manor house. I brought my nan along, and she later adopted the most adorable pound puppy, a mostly black tricolor Chihuahua we call Paisley.

Somewhere along the way, our gang realized we had a knack for solving mysteries and started up an official business, which—much to my chagrin—has been dubbed Pet Whisperer P.I. The last thing I want is strangers knowing I can talk to animals, but luckily they all seem to think our moniker is a joke or some misguided publicity attempt.

Whatever the case, they're always happy once we get the job done. Admittedly, most of our cases are unpaid. And usually we're not even formally hired. Mysteries just fall into our laps, and well, what else are we going to do to fill our days?

I don't take kindly to being called an amateur sleuth, mind you. I have an official business with a registered LLC and everything. That makes me a professional, thank you very much.

My fiancé is the senior partner at a local law firm—the same one I used to work at. That place saw tons of turnover until Charles took his place at the top. Now things are nice and steady, and together the two of us make up the small-town Maine version of *Law and Order*.

The last prominent member of our quirky ensemble is our very own trash panda, Pringle. He's a sticky-fingered raccoon who lives in a treehouse out back. He likes cat food and Nerf guns, but he loves reality TV. Most of the time he causes more problems than he solves, but we love him anyway. Well, most of us do.

Even after more than a year together, I'm pretty sure I only register as "kind of like" on my cat's affection scale, and Pringle ranks much, much lower.

Me? I've got all the love I can handle between planning a wedding and getting to know the bio grandmother I recently reconnected with after a lifetime of not even knowing she existed. The best part? My Grandma Lyn can talk to animals too, and believe me you, we've talked about our shared talents until we were both blue in the face.

Nan still feels a little jealous, but she's working on it. I could meet a hundred long-lost relatives and would still never turn my back on the woman who raised me and in the process became my very best friend.

As much as I'm looking forward to tying the knot with Charles, a small part of me is dreading it too. I've lived with Nan almost my entire life— the whole thing excluding a brief period when I tried to establish independence in a crummy rental. Marrying Charles means I'll be moving in with him, and Nan has made it clear that we newlyweds should be granted our space when the time comes.

I guess for now I'll soak up every second with my funny, sunny grandmother. It's not like we'll be moving far away. In fact, I won't be moving at all. Nan has decided to buy her old house back from Charles—what a lucky turn of events that he bought her old place when she moved in with me at Octo-Cat's manor house—and Charles will move in here with me. It's a short drive and one we're all already used to making on the regular.

Things won't be so bad. Just different. I've already told Nan to expect me over for dinner at least five times per week, and I also plan to keep her room exactly as it is in case she ever decides to move back. She's not getting any younger, though I swear she's in better shape than me and will likely outlive us all... even Octo-Cat, who has nine lives to lose before he's through.

* * *

Normally I wake up to the smell of Nan's fresh baked goods wafting from the kitchen. Today, however, a sharp pain on my chest lurched me from sleep.

"Confess or die!" Pringle shouted and sent Paisley scampering over my chest once more.

"Stop! You're scaring me!" the little Chihuahua yipped, tucking her tail tight beneath her as she ran.

"You're scaring us all, kiddo. That's what happens when you keep secrets from the fuzz." Now the raccoon was sitting firmly on my chest as if I were some kind of soapbox for his ridiculous speech. His claws were sharp, and it hurt.

"Pringle," I growled and shoved him off me. "You're not supposed to be in the house, and you're especially not supposed to be in my room."

"Sorry, toots. Didn't mean to wake ya, but you're harboring my main suspect, and that won't do." He shook a little black finger in the air. "There's no hiding from the long arm of the law!"

"But I don't even have arms!" Paisley cried. "I'm a dog. I only have legs!"

Pringle slapped his hand into his forehead and

sighed heavily. "Dick Tracy never had to deal with this, I can assure you."

I wasn't sure whether he was talking to me, himself, or an imaginary audience. Whatever the case, I was done with this whole thing. Ever since our resident raccoon developed a taste for old back-and-white gumshoe films, we'd all been short on rest. Lately, he turned everything into a case to be solved. Yesterday we were all treated to the case of "Why is the water bowl empty?" Admittedly, that one was pretty open and shut; Pringle spent more time recounting the glory of his victory than he did investigating.

"Go play somewhere else." I pulled the blanket over my head, praying that this time they might actually listen.

Paisley slipped under the comforter and licked the inside of my ear. "Mommy!" she squeaked so loud it sent me bolt upright. "Pringle says it's my fault there's a big truck outside. He said I've been feeding secrets to the Russians. But I don't even know who that is or why they're in such a hurry."

It was way, way too early for this. Unfortunately, past experience dictated there was no way I'd be getting back to sleep. Besides, poor Paisley had always been too easy of a target for Pringle. He would stay on her until I forcibly split the two of them up.

I groaned and swung my feet to the floor. "Pringle, you are not allowed in my bedroom. Not in the morning. Not ever. Understood?"

"Yeah, I understand. The cat and dog are allowed in, but just because I'm a raccoon..." He threw his arms up in the air. "That's profiling. Just because I've got a mask and rings on my tail. Frankly, I didn't take you for the type."

"Outdoor animals need to stay outdoors," I eked out between clenched teeth.

"Whoa, whoa, whoa, sweetheart. Do you even hear yourself?" Something lit in his eyes, and he laughed. "Oh, I get it. This isn't about me at all."

"It's not?"

"No, you're threatened by my investigative prowess. I get it. A failed P.I. like you? Of course you're threatened by a brilliant ingenue such as myself."

"Excuse me," I thundered, then chased the little bandit out of my tower, down two flights of stairs, and through the electronic pet door, which somehow he'd managed to hack once again.

Paisley ran behind me, barking the whole way.

"And stay out, you no-good doodoo head!" she ruffed before bolting through the pet door herself.

I pulled back the drapes to watch the two of them fly through the yard where, sure enough, an enormous moving truck stood idling in our driveway.

DEER DUPLICITY is now available.

Get your copy so that you can keep reading this series today!

ABOUT MOLLY FITZ

While *USA Today bestselling* author Molly Fitz can't technically talk to animals, she and her three feline writing assistants have deep and very animated conversations as they navigate their days.

She lives with her child and their own private zoo somewhere in the wilds of Alaska. Molly will occasionally venture out for good food, great coffee, or to meet new animal friends.

Learn more about Molly and her books, and be sure to sign up for her newsletter at **www.Molly Mysteries.com**.

ALSO BY MOLLY FITZ

Learn more about Molly's collected works, so that you can decide which book you'd like to read next...

PET WHISPERER P.I.

Angie Russo just partnered up with Blueberry Bay's first ever talking cat detective. Along with his ragtag gang of human and animal helpers, Octo-Cat is determined to save the day... so long as it doesn't interfere with his schedule.

Start with book 1, *Kitty Confidential*.

MERLIN'S MAGICAL MYSTERIES

Gracie Springs is not a witch... but her cat is. Now she must help to keep his secret or risk spending the rest of her life in some magical prison. Too bad trouble seems to find them at every turn!

Start with book 1, *Merlin Takes a Familiar*.

PARANORMAL TEMP AGENCY

Tawny Bigford's simple life takes a turn for the magical when she stumbles upon her landlady's murder and is recruited by a talking black cat named Fluffikins to take over the deceased's role as the official Town Witch for Beech Grove, Georgia.

Start with book 1, *Witch for Hire*.

THE MYSTERIES OF MOONLIGHT MANOR (WITH TRIXIE SILVERTALE)

Sydney Coleman has it all—until she doesn't. No sooner does she launch her bed and breakfast, than a trio of ghosts turn up oppose her at every turn. They insist she solve the murder of their mistress, but Sydney is desperate for cash. If she can't book some guests fast, her haunted mansion is utterly doomed.

Start with book 1, ***Moonlight & Mischief***.

CONNECT WITH MOLLY

Sign up for my newsletter and get a special digital prize pack for joining, including an exclusive story, *Meowy Christmas Mayhem*, fun quiz, and lots of cat pictures!

Sign up: **MollyMysteries.com/subscribe**

Now, if you ever wished you could converse with cats, here's your opportunity! This is me officially inviting you into my whacky inner world as part of my Cozy Kitty Book Club.

For those who just can't get enough of my zany cat characters and their hapless humans, this book club will provide new content to devour and the chance to get to know my best author friends.

From exclusive stories, behind-the-scenes trivia to never-before-released bonus content, and monthly giveaways, there's a lot to love about the Cozy Kitty Book Club. Join today to find out what we're reading next!

Join: **MollyMysteries.com/club**